The Life of Colin Phelps

The Life of Colin Phelps

A Novel By:

Kevin Kelley

Cloondahamper West Publications

Published by Cloondahamper West Publications

ISBN 978-1-0992-3915-1

Typesetting services by BOOKOW.COM

London, 1855

The cobblestones felt cold and damp under Colin's thin knees as he crept quietly under the flower stand. It wasn't open yet. The vendor wouldn't arrive for another twenty minutes, so it provided good cover as the boy approached a bread cart from behind.

Stealth was a talent Colin had fashioned into a true art form. By his tenth birthday, he'd learned to be invisible, knew how to sneak in and out of almost any building, how to find food in any season.

He watched a large horse-drawn carriage approaching, knowing it would distract the baker, timing his moment. The vendor never noticed the boy's swift actions as he helped himself to an armful of freshly baked goods.

Pigeons took flight around him as he turned and darted down a stone stairway to the river. He felt they were escaping together, wished he could fly.

On his right, a barge drifted slowly down the Thames, its stove lit at center deck. He inhaled the scent of coffee and bacon from onboard and watched men warming their hands by its fire.

Colin had that thought again. Someday, I'll ride down the Thames and board a ship to Australia or New Zealand. Maybe even America.

He slowed to a brisk walk, glanced over his shoulder, breathed in the rich warm odor of fresh-baked bread, and bit into the end of a loaf, savoring its taste.

Day by day, Colin made it through the winter of 1855, subsisting on what he could steal and on dreams of ocean voyages. His father had gone to sea years ago on a trading vessel bound for New York. The boy didn't understand why he hadn't returned, why he wasn't there when his mother died. Sometimes he looked expectantly at ships as they approached. Mostly, he resented them and fumed at being alone.

Ships had their own perils, of course. Just last year, the RMS Tayleur wrecked off the coast of Ireland. Its compass, thrown off by a new metal hull, sent her dangerously off course. Of her 650 passengers and crew, only 290 survived. Colin tried not to think of ships sinking, but he'd heard the story often from the crews of lightermen who unloaded cargo on the river. He hoped to join their profession, but an apprenticeship required a sponsor, which he could never attain. Colin couldn't understand that; the unfairness of it.

He liked being with them at first. A few weren't much older than him, but most were grown men. They told stories, gambled, drank with enthusiasm, and occasionally shared a few goods that had "fallen from the boat."

They could also be dangerous. He learned to be vigilant, keeping a safe distance, always planning an escape route to scramble away when fights broke out. Competition with other crews was a growing concern.

A team from a different barge would suddenly appear, brandishing clubs and leather switches, with each claiming their right to offload certain ships and each fighting fiercely until the claim was resolved. Both sides lost men to serious bodily injury but, so far, none died.

They all fared better than Colin's mother. She died of cholera in the Broad Street epidemic the previous year. Colin's father was still away at sea, or worse. His ship should have returned a year ago, but never had. Colin cursed his father the night he watched his mother slip away.

When her illness worsened, he begged the landlord to fetch Doctor Miller, but even he was too ill to venture out. There was no hope any of them would see a physician. Medical staff was overwhelmed with the sick and dying. Bodies were being loaded onto carts every day.

Colin sat with his mother, wiping the sweat from her face and forehead as she moaned and shook. He didn't understand why she wasn't getting better. In a panic, he ran across the hall, knocking on Mrs. Culver's door, begging for help. Her shouted curses echoed through the hallway, yelling at him to leave her alone. Colin raced downstairs to the flat on the first floor. No one answered. He banged on the door until his knuckles bled and tears fell from his eyes.

Back at her bedside, in a darkening room lit by only one thin candle, he made up what he thought was a good-sounding prayer and repeated it earnestly over and over, out loud, until his voice was gone. He watched helplessly as the energy drained from her body, and she perished in just over eight hours.

After she died, he knelt silently at her bedside, weeping, his head face down on her covers, trembling. The shadow of his kneeling body climbed high up the wall. He felt small, completely alone, hopeless, and afraid.

Colin developed a fever, too, but didn't care. He hoped he would die so he could join her in heaven. Maybe he couldn't, maybe there isn't a heaven, or a God. If there is, he certainly doesn't answer prayers.

His own illness grew grotesquely. No one was there to comfort him as his fever spiked. His mother lay cold and still in her bed, while he sweated and vomited and moaned on his mattress.

Sometime long into the next day, his temperature subsided, and he fell into a deep sleep that lasted several hours. All alone, Colin pulled through, needing to deal with his mother's body when he woke.

He stood silently at her bedside, not sure what to do, then gingerly folded her arms across her chest, refusing to look at her vacant eyes. Colin covered her with the colorful quilt she always cherished, then slowly opened the door, giving her one last long look, before closing it gently, quietly, reverently as he went to find help. Four hours elapsed before two men, dressed entirely in black, and a small woman hidden under a thick dark veil, came to take her away. The woman gave his mother's body a perfunctory look then held out her thin boney hand.

"The amount we agreed to … and the quilt."

Colin started to protest but stopped when the larger man stepped forward. He took a wooden chair and dragged it to the tall wardrobe near the window. The chair creaked and swayed as he stepped up and lifted himself on to tiptoes. He felt along the top of the cupboard and retrieved a brightly painted biscuit tin. The illustration on the lid celebrated Queen Victoria's coronation twenty years before, another of the few items his mother prized.

He opened it and withdrew the eight pounds she kept there. "For rainy days," she'd said, "if it can get any wetter than this." He hadn't known what she meant until now. Colin handed the money to the woman, but clutched the tin and held it fast to his chest as she reached to grab it.

He watched, speechless, afraid to cry. They refused to let him follow. "Too much risk of disease." Colin went to the window and watched as the men laid his mother on the back of a long wagon. One of them pulled the quilt off her body, and his mother's blank eyes stared up at him. Colin stepped back, swallowed hard, then moved closer, placing both hands on the glass, watching until the wagon was out of sight. He turned to look at the drab empty room, sat on the only upholstered chair, and sobbed.

On His Own

THREE days later, the landlord threw him out. Colin had a vague recollection of an aunt and uncle, perhaps cousins, living at Tewkesbury. But he had no way of contacting them. He couldn't read or write and had no idea where Tewkesbury was.

He had more immediate concerns, his only possessions being the clothes on his back, his mother's wedding ring and a few items in her biscuit tin he managed to grab before being locked out. He'd barely eaten in two days and didn't know where he'd find his next meal.

That's when Colin stole his first food: two green apples from a fruit stand and a sausage link he ate raw. He spent the night inside St. Anne's Church, sleeping under a back pew. The church was pitch black. It was August, but the stone floor felt cool.

The church was famous for its choir and organ music. It was that instrument that startled Colin out of a deep sleep. The organist prepared for service by playing loud trumpeting chords. The boy curled into a ball, covering his ears, assaulted by the sound. Once recovered, he snuck out, afraid of being found. He felt a sharp pang of guilt over stealing his supper. God might not answer prayers, but he might be vengeful. Colin thought it best to avoid churches after that.

He spent the autumn months pillaging what food he could and sleeping under bushes in Regent's Park or Hyde Park. As winter set in, he learned ways into and out of buildings. Sometimes, he would sleep in stables near the horses for warmth. Sometimes, the railway station offered cover when he wasn't chased away by vigilant stationmasters.

Winter was nearly done now. Colin was filthy, cold, and urgently hungry. He spent the night in a warehouse just off the docks, sneaking in before closing and hiding behind a stack of barrels until the workmen went home. They locked the doors behind them.

That didn't bother Colin. Locks are meant to keep people from getting in. Once inside, there was usually a way out. This building, however, was secure. There were no windows, no rooftop exits. The large carriage doors at one end appeared to have been padlocked from the outside, and the smaller door on the other side was locked tight. He barely slept. Cold, and fear of discovery, intruded on his sleep.

At daybreak, both carriage doors opened wide with a sharp screeching sound. A horse-drawn wagon rode right up to the barrels. His heart beat quickly as he crouched to the ground. The horse's head protruded above the barrels, emitting heavy gusts of steam that touched Colin's face.

He held his breath and thought of excuses. Usually, he could talk his way out of trouble with convincing stories but was too tired to craft a good one this time. They would likely beat him, search his pockets, and throw him into the street. Someone shouted from the entrance as the workmen dismounted, "We're needed on the wharf." Both men ambled out, and Colin took full advantage to make his escape.

Seagulls shrieked and swooped along the water's edge, searching for food. He smelled the rot of garbage floating on the Thames. The moon on the horizon cast a thin shaft of light onto the water as brisk wind picked up, blowing cold air through Colin's thin coat. His pockets provided little protection for bare hands that were already numb.

London's fish market would open soon. He could earn breakfast by being among the first at dockside to unload the evening's catch. It was hard, messy work. Colin's trembling hands grew wetter and more frigid as he handled the slippery fish and tossed them on to wagons. Their scales scratched and cut his fingers.

When it was done, he was covered with the pungent odor of fish. But he had earned thick slices of rye bread, a bowl of hot chowder, and a mug of tea, each of which he held with shivering, oily hands.

Captured

With his hunger slightly controlled, he turned to his main goal for the day: warmer clothing. It required stealth, but he knew a market where a little speed and distraction could accomplish his purpose.

It should be easy. He'd "shopped" there before. The flea market was adjacent to Hanover Square. Its wares were mostly used, mostly lower quality, but they would be warm. Colin walked around the stalls twice, weaving through the crowd, eyeing each of the carts and each of the sellers. Some vendors were vigilant. Others spent more time talking with their neighbors or watching their children. Children were supposed to attract buyers, but in fact, they tended to wander and play, so they demanded a good deal of attention from their parents.

A thick gray scarf and a pair of woolen gloves lay on a corner of one cart: easy pickings. Colin passed by, looking casually in the opposite direction as his hand deftly reached with one swift action, cupping the scarf and gloves, swiping them under his coat.

He'd barely taken ten steps when a firm hand grabbed the back of his neck. Colin struggled, but the grip was too tight. Another hand took solid hold of his coat just above his left shoulder. It was impossible to get free. The hands steered him up against a cold brick wall and pinned him there.

"Well, what have we got here?" a voice asked.

"Lemme go … Get yer hands off o' me!"

"Not so fast. Do you know stealing is a sin? That it's an offense to God?"

"God don't exist or, if he does, he don't care a fig fer anything I do."

"Is that so, boy?"

The grip eased slightly, and Colin could turn part way around, surprised to discover he was in the grasp of a large, imposing priest.

"What's your name, lad?"

"Let me be. I ain't hurt'n' no one."

"Taking what doesn't belong to you is taking food off another man's table. It's a serious transgression, my son."

"It's just to keep warm. I'm freezing. Please let go o' me."

"I might, or I might turn you over to the authorities. Tell me your name, child."

"I'm just a boy ..."

"A boy with a name, I presume?"

"Colin."

"Well, Colin, do your parents know you steal?"

"M' parents are gone, taken by cholera and the ocean. Please let me go."

"Is that so? How old are you, boy?"

"Nearly eleven."

"Tell me, Colin, can you read and write?"

"No, sir." He squirmed but couldn't get free.

"Can you figure with numbers?"

"A little." The priest relaxed his grip a bit more.

"Well, you've barely any talents at all. It seems thievery is your only skill. Do you know music?'"

"Music?"

"Do you play an instrument? Can you sing?"

Colin certainly couldn't play an instrument. He'd never seen a sheet of music and did not know if he could sing.

People were acknowledging the priest, pausing to stare, wondering what was happening. He was obviously well-known and respected. Colin was sure a bobby would arrive any moment and the priest would turn him in with the ill-gotten goods under his coat. But the priest seemed keen on this whole music business.

"We've a Boys Choir at my church. Can you sing scales?" he asked.

Colin knew fish had scales. Other than that, he didn't know what the priest was asking. He stared dumbfounded at the cleric.

"Sing after me," the priest said. And then he sang a set of scales. Colin didn't move. So the priest sang them again. "Just like that."

Colin cleared his throat and softly repeated the notes.

"Stronger," the priest implored. "Again." He raised one arm from the elbow as if conducting an orchestra. Colin repeated the notes a bit more forcefully.

"Yes. Again. Louder!"

Colin felt embarrassed, but it seemed to take the priest's mind off the stolen goods. So he raised his voice and sang the notes again. Each note was clear, distinct, and perfectly on key. The priest held him at arm's length and looked earnestly into his eyes.

"Saints be praised. You're a gift from God, my son!"

Colin seriously doubted that. But the priest was excited, almost exuberant.

"How would you like a proper meal and a safe, warm place to live?"

"Please sir, I won't steal again. Can I go now?"

"I'm in earnest, lad. My name's Father McCall. I run the school and the choir at St. Anne's church. You'd be welcome to stay with us. We'll teach you to read and write, even learn arithmetic and Latin. You'll not go hungry, never have to steal again. You will be a marvelous addition to our choir."

Colin remembered sleeping on the floor of the church and didn't want to go back but decided to play along. He could escape when the priest relaxed.

Father McCall smiled and held his large right hand out for several seconds. Colin stared at him, confused, then realized what the priest meant and slipped his hand under his coat, pulling the stolen clothing out and placing them in the priest's hand.

"Donovan," the priest called to the merchant, "it seems some items fell off your cart."

The merchant looked appreciatively at the priest and smiled but paused as realization took hold, and he gave Colin a look of contempt.

Father McCall kept his thick hand on Colin's shoulder, guiding him toward St. Anne's. He explained the church could provide education to a child, boy or girl, who couldn't afford to pay. Wealthy benefactors blessed the church. His genuine excitement radiated when he spoke of the Boys Choir, which he explained was famous throughout all of England.

"We've performed for royalty and for the highest levels of the church. Cardinals requested St. Anne's choir for the installment of bishops and the marriages of lords. Prime Ministers requested them for the opening of Parliament."

"I don't know any proper songs." He actually knew a few tunes with vulgar language he'd never repeat to a priest.

"You will, son. You will. But first you'll eat. Do you like lamb stew, lad?"

Colin remained apprehensive. He had strong memories of false kindness and betrayals.

"Yes, but I've no place in church or school. I'm not the sort to benefit from such as that."

"You're exactly the sort, and precisely the type of boy our parishioners want to help. I suspect you are as bright or brighter than many of our students. You just need a guiding hand. The Lord has a purpose for you, son."

He escorted Colin up the steps of the church and through a long hallway leading to a staircase that descended to a large open room set up with rows of writing desks and chairs. Their footsteps echoed off the walls.

"This is part of the school. You'll see all of it after you eat."

At the far end of the room, another hallway led to the dining area. Colin smelled fresh bread and the savory odor of roasted lamb. He realized he'd not eaten a real supper since his mother died. He would certainly stay through the meal.

A generous portion of stew was ladled into a large bowl. Bread, still warm from the oven, was in a basket, accompanied by a jar of orange marmalade, and tea was served in a hand-painted porcelain cup. Colin ate until he could barely move. His stomach ached, unaccustomed to such bounty.

St. Anne's School

"Now it's time to get you clean. When's the last time you had a proper bath, a hot bath with soap?"

Colin couldn't remember the last time he'd experienced a hot bath. At this point, he wasn't sure he ever had. If so, it was a long, long time ago. He shrugged his shoulders in an "I don't know" response.

"Well, you're certainly due for one. Way past due in fact." Father McCall crossed the room and pulled on a long piece of velvet roping hanging from the ceiling. A bell sounded faintly in another room and was soon followed by the appearance of an overweight woman in her late fifties, wearing a starched uniform and a look of complete efficiency.

"We've a new student, Millicent, a songbird for our choir. He'll look less like a crow, I'll wager, once all the dirt is scrubbed free. Please draw him a bath and see to his uniform."

Millicent looked at the boy with apprehension, then led him along the stone corridor to the large arched wooden door at the end. It opened onto a grass courtyard. A statue of a woman stood in the center, surrounded by a raised stone flowerbed. In spring, the bed would burst with bright pink tulips and yellow daffodils under saintly white roses. But now the winter rosebushes looked lonely, sparse, and weary.

"That is our Saint," Millicent said. "Saint Anne, the mother of our Blessed Virgin. She's the protector of women and children. I suspect she brought you here to us."

Colin started to say it was thievery that brought him here. He doubted that stealing a scarf and gloves would have attracted the attention of a saint. But instead, he just said, “Yes, ma’am.”

They crossed the courtyard, entering a building almost as large as the church. Its base was constructed of stone up to the first floor. Above that, it was encased by wooden slats and topped off with a high-pitched shingled roof. Small windows gaped haphazardly along its walls. Two solid brick chimneys, billowing smoke, squeezed the building from both sides.

The door opened to a dim hallway bisecting the building, with rooms on either side. A narrow wooden staircase stood just inside the entrance. In the low light, it was difficult to tell if the stairs led straight up or curved as they reached their height. Millicent lit a kerosene lantern from the table by the door.

“Up you go,” she said.

He started up the squeaking steps. Millicent held the lantern as she followed behind. With the light at his back, Colin strained to see his way forward. His shoulders brushed the walls on both sides. He smelled a mixture of odors: smoke, sweat, and musty clothes.

The second floor consisted of a large dormitory with cots lining the walls on either side. Fragile-looking wooden trunks stood at the foot of each cot. Some were open, revealing clothes, books and, in one, a violin. Colin wondered if a violin might fetch a good price.

An aisle between the cots led back to a large door, which opened to a bathing room. Three large metal tubs sat in the middle. A fireplace at the end heated the room as well as the water for the tubs. Millicent instructed him to fill buckets and heat them before filling his tub.

“A pious person holds himself clean and spotless in the eyes of the Lord. God looks to us to care for the gifts he has given us. We must be arduous in our devotion, industrious in our labors, and disciplined in all our endeavors. The human body is a temple to the Lord and should be treated accordingly.”

Colin desperately wanted her to leave. But she droned on and on about the grace of St. Anne, the purity of the church, and devotion to God.

When his tub was filled, he looked to her to as if to say, "I am ready. You can go now." But she stayed and insisted he undress. Colin moved so the tub was between them, offering a small amount of modesty. He turned his back and undid his buttons, kicked off his shoes, and slowly removed his trousers. When he was down to his ragged undershorts, he stepped into the tub. Millicent noticed he wore a leather string around his neck. At the end of it was his mother's wedding ring.

Millicent took a towel from a rack and used it to gather up his clothes so she wouldn't have to touch them with her hands.

"Not even fit for the orphanage," she mumbled.

She handed Colin a bar of soap and instructed him to "clean every crease and crevasse.

"I'll be back with a proper outfit." She bustled out of the room, the floorboards moaning and squeaking as she crossed back through the dormitory.

Colin conceded a hot bath felt good. His bones had been cold for so long. After scrubbing, he sank into the tub and laid his head against the edge, closing his eyes, enjoying the warmth of the water, and wondering what his mother would think.

Suddenly, a loud circus of voices erupted downstairs. He heard laughter and shouting, and the sound of shoes running up the steps. He looked frantically for some place to hide.

There was a towel on a rack by the window. He got out of the tub, slipped badly, falling on his side, then hurried to regain his footing, grabbing the towel, and wrapping it around him just as the door burst open.

A thin boy about Colin's age burst in, still laughing at something that happened outside.

"Hello. What's this?" he said, staring wide-eyed at Colin. "You're new. Who're you?"

Colin felt as if he been caught stealing at the market again. "The priest sent me up here. That woman, Millicent, made me wash."

"Did old Millie give you a good scrubbing herself?"

"No. She took my clothes. I don't know where she's gone."

"Hey fellows," the boy yelled, "look what we've got here! Father seems to have adopted another one."

Boys began squeezing into the room. One of the larger students pushed his way forward and gave Colin a long calculating stare.

"What's your name?"

"Colin."

"Father's always bringing in strays. Where'd he find you?"

Before he could answer, Millicent returned, holding clothes under her arm.

"Out!" she shouted. "Out! Let the boy dress, and then we can all be introduced."

As they were heading out, the larger boy stopped and fixed a covetous gaze on the ring around Colin's neck.

Millicent carefully placed the clothes on a chair. "This is the St. Anne's uniform. It signifies you are a pupil of our school, that you have a place in the world. Boys have worn this uniform since our school was founded in 1699. Girls are admitted as well, beginning in 1704. They are in Montclair House. I myself am a graduate of St Anne's.

"Wearing our uniform carries a solemn responsibility to conduct oneself with dignity and honor. We are devoted to elevating society to its highest level, in keeping with the teachings of our Lord. You will find we care for the poor, for widows and orphans, for those who struggle under unjust labor, or who live in squalor."

He wondered if she ever stopped talking.

"Our Blessed Mother may have found no room at the inn, but you have a place with us. You must never bring dishonor to the good name of St. Anne's Parish."

Colin feared she'd stay and watch him dress. To his relief she said, "Empty the tub and take care to clean it. When you're properly attired, I'll introduce you to your mates." She twirled around and strode efficiently out the door, the floorboards again testifying to her departure.

The clothes were new. Undershorts, a white shirt, a blue sweater with an insignia over the left breast, gray pants, gray socks, and, to his amazement, a pair of shoes with laces. There was a necktie with the school's colors. He hadn't the faintest idea how to tie it so left it off. He felt strange. Clean, well dressed, but strange. Colin took a deep breath and slowly opened the door.

The others had forgotten him for a time and were lounging on cots or grouped in conversation. When the door opened, he immediately attracted attention. They approached, encircling him.

The same larger boy asserted his presence. "New boys have to earn privileges," he said. "Where'd Father find you?"

"Hanover Square."

"Odd. You look more like a river rat to me. I'm Blaine. If you behave yourself and do as I tell you, you'll be fine. But if you get out of line …"

Colin didn't have any intention of letting Blaine, or anyone else, run his life.

Millicent spoke up. "Blaine is too full of himself, Colin. Everyone, this is Colin. Colin what's your last name?"

"Phelps."

"Well then, Colin Phelps, everyone! Father tells me he will join our choir. Colin's an orphan. I expect you all to show Christian charity to help him feel at home."

She took the tie from Colin's hand, wrapped it around his neck, and secured it in a quick, efficient manner. "Must always wear the uniform properly, always with pride."

Turning to the address the room, she added, “You students have quiet time now to work on your studies before supper.” She gestured toward a cot close to the staircase. “This is yours, Colin. I hope you enjoy your stay with us.”

After she left, Blaine gave Colin a long, domineering stare before returning to his cot to read. The first boy who encountered Colin in the bath approached.

“I’m Malcolm. Good to have you here. Be wary of Blaine. He fancies himself king of the roost.”

“He’s not king of me, and never will be.”

“Nevertheless, use caution around him.”

“I will. Thanks. How long you been here?”

“It’s my third year. Most boys have families who pay for their schooling. But I’m an orphan like you. My family died in a fire. My mum and sister died in their beds. Dad pulled me out just before the fire exploded. When he couldn’t get back inside, he ran to the stable to save our horse. He never came out. Two of our neighbors lost their homes that night. But my family was the only one lost. St. Anne’s has been my home ever since.”

“I’m not an orphan, not yet anyway. My father went to sea, but I know he’ll come back someday soon. How’s it here? What’s this place really like?”

“It’s good. We scrap amongst ourselves, but Father McCall keeps us in line and provides for us. You can put your belongings in your chest.” He motioned toward trunk at the end of Colin’s cot.

“I haven’t any possessions.”

He actually had a few treasured items hidden under a wharf in his mother’s tin, held beneath the dock by lengths of leather strapping. It consisted of some marbles, a toy soldier, three of his mother’s ribbons, and a letter he couldn’t read. He knew his father had written it to his mother. She had told him it was good news; their lives would change for the better. But that was over four months before she died.

Nothing had changed. Life only got worse. Colin was waiting to find someone he could trust to read it to him.

Colin brought his left fingers up to the knot of his tie and tugged, while the fingers of his right hand slid under the collar and stretched it out. "Must we wear these things?"

"You'll get used to in time. Here, I'll help you tie it."

First Night

THREE hours later a bell rang. The boys hurried to line up at the top of the stairs. Blaine strode to the head of the line while the others yielded position to him.

Colin followed as the students tromped down the stairs, across the courtyard, and into the basement of the church. They entered a large dining hall with long tables running the length of the room. Wooden benches ran along both sides of the tables.

Boys stood behind them like soldiers at attention. Colin wondered why they weren't sitting down. He saw another table at the front with Father McCall, Millicent, another priest, and young adults he assumed were teachers.

Father McCall raised his arms as a signal for the room to be still. When all was quiet, he began: "Heavenly Father, bless this food to the nourishment of our bodies and us to Thy service. May we always be mindful of the needs of others. In Christ's name, we pray. Amen."

The boys all uttered a perfunctory "Amen," then quickly took their seats. A pewter plate and cup sat at each place on the table. Bowls of steaming potatoes, plates of string beans, and platters of white fish sat at various places, along with baskets of bread and pitchers of milk. Colin noticed Blaine was first to grab the fish. He overfilled his plate without caring what would be left for others. Another boy was reaching for the potatoes when Blaine grabbed the bowl from his hands. No one offered objections.

The plates were passed along the table. By the time they reached Colin he was left with only a sliver of fish and two small potatoes.

But the bread and milk were plentiful. He wasn't hungry anyway, after his large lunch.

Toward the end of supper Father McCall stood and clinked his cup loudly with a fork. "I've an announcement," he said. "We have a new student. Colin Phelps will be with us and will join our choir. Choirmaster Thompson, I think you'll find him a welcome addition to your alto section. I ask you all to extend Christian kindness to young Colin and welcome him into our school. Colin, please stand to be greeted."

To Colin's surprise the boys applauded, and most gave him smiles and nods of encouragement. He hadn't said he would join the choir. He didn't know if he would stay. Still, this might not be such a bad place after all.

Students remained seated when supper was done. Choirmaster Thompson rose and rang a large silver bell. The boys all stood. Thompson raised his right arm to conduct. He mouthed, "One, two, three."

The boys sang,

"Praise God, from whom all blessings flow.

Praise Him all creatures here below."

Four more verses followed until they sang,

Amen. Amen. Amen."

While it was clear the boys weren't enthusiastic about the hymn, Colin was stunned by the quality of their voices. Notes floated like crystals in the air, clean and clear, exalted. It was as though the dining hall was now a great cathedral. Even the gas lanterns along the wall seemed to glow brighter.

He began to understand what the priest had bragged about. His emotions ranged from hope on one hand to fear he would never fit in on the other.

That night Colin slept in an actual bed beneath a warm blanket with a pillow under his head for the first time in over a year. Before turning down the lanterns, the boys knelt beside their beds, under the watchful eye of Father Gustave, and recited,

"Now I lay me down to sleep,
I pray the Lord my soul to keep.
Thy angels watch me through the night,
And keep me safe till morning's light."

Colin couldn't tell if they were sincere or not. They were certainly different from the boys he knew from the streets and the wharfs. He planned to stay awake, perhaps he'd sneak out when the others were asleep, but events of the day descended heavily upon him.

He drifted into a deep, clear dream of his mother and father at a picnic. They were sitting in a garden under a clear blue sky, surrounded by flowers and blossoming fruit trees, the air infused with the scent of honeysuckles. Colin watched them but wasn't with them. They smiled and laughed while his mother talked about the dress she would wear to their wedding.

His father took both her hands into his and kissed them saying, "I take these hands and only these, for evermore in marriage."

In his dream, Colin called out to them. They turned but didn't see him. He called louder, but they went back to laughing and talking with one another. Why wouldn't they hear him? His last yell woke him.

Malcolm came to his bedside.

"Hey, are you awake? What's wrong?"

In the seconds it took to realize where he was, that he'd only been dreaming, Colin felt embarrassed, afraid he'd woken others. To his relief, everyone other than Malcolm remained sound asleep.

"You were having a nightmare."

He thought for a second, trying to hold the dream.

"No, it was a good dream. It was my parents." But the images were slipping from his memory. "I'm fine. Didn't mean to wake you."

"It's all right. You're safe now. Go back to sleep."

Rude Awakening

Loud clanging of a heavy metal bell startled Colin from his dreams. Father Gustav strode briskly down the corridor between cots nearly singing, "Another day the Lord has made! Time for prayer, m' lads."

Colin scrunched into a fetal position, clutching his blanket tight around him. The bell jangled louder. Colin realized the priest stood directly over him shaking the bell for all it was worth. "No dallying, boy. Your Savior awaits."

He flopped onto his side, draping his arm across his ear, snarling something unintelligible. Father Gustav responded by ripping the blanket off him and smiling angelically as he said, "You don't want to keep the other boys waiting on your first day, do you?"

Colin sat up, scowling at the cleric as he swung his feet onto the floor. His hand reached instinctively to his mother's ring hanging from his neck, then he turned from the bell ringer, vowing to run away after breakfast.

The students gathered at the top of the stairs. Blaine shoulder-bumped Colin from behind and then ambled confidently to the front, his hands in his pockets, leading the procession.

Colin stood staring at the back of Blaine's head before joining the end of the line. He thought they were heading to the dining hall, but they proceeded out across the courtyard and into the church. Father McCall stood at the altar, waiting to lead them in morning prayers.

He watched the others and mimicked their actions. He had often heard his mother in prayer and remembered the night she suffered, praying softly between coughs and shivers until her soul left her body. Prayer was meaningful to her. She taught him one to say at bedtime, but it differed from what these boys recited.

He felt awkward, yet something about the reverence, the stained-glass windows, flickering candles, and the warmth of the church made him feel close to her again, almost a feeling of home.

When the final "Amen" was said, the boys filed out to the center aisle and streamed to the door of the church. Father McCall preceded them and stood addressing several by name, smiling and encouraging each one. As Colin reached the door, the priest put his arm on his shoulder, said how glad he was to have him in the school, and told him Deacon Prentiss would meet him after breakfast to assess his skills. Colin wasn't sure what that meant.

Breakfast was more generous than Colin expected: milk and tea, oranges, fresh rolls, and hot porridge with cinnamon. "Perhaps," he thought, "I should wait until after lunch to escape."

With breakfast done, the students assembled for announcements from the headmaster, then filed out to their respective classes. Colin followed, but McCall pulled him aside.

"Time to find out what's in that brain of yours. Come with me." He guided him down a narrow hall to a brightly lit room where a gangly man sat on a piano bench, his left elbow resting on the instrument, supporting his head as he gently fingered the keys with his right hand.

"Here's the protégé I promised you, Prentiss. I'm looking forward to your report."

Prentiss stood, extending a hand for the boy to shake. Colin stepped back. He watched as the man unfolded himself, rising until he towered over the boy like an enormous thin-legged crane staring down at him. Prentiss was the tallest man the boy had ever seen. His thin face was topped with a fire of red hair, and his pale blue eyes peered at him over the rim of large round spectacles. A fastidious man smelling of powder.

"Don't be afraid, lad. I'm perfectly harmless. Just want to know what skills you've acquired before joining us. Please sit down." He removed his glasses and gestured with them toward a row of chairs. "Sit. We'll just have a little talk. Have you attended school before?"

"No, sir."

"And why is that?"

Colin shifted in his chair, turning his head to take in every part of the room, looking for another exit. He was embarrassed at not having been in school, worried he might have to account for his life on the street, and angry this giraffe should be asking him questions. He stared back at Prentiss blankly.

"I understand your parents are gone. That must be very hard on you. Have you any brothers or sisters?"

"No."

"Well, we're like a large family here. You'll find we take care of each other. Was your breakfast good?"

Colin nodded impatiently, his right leg bouncing, his heel tapping the floor.

"I'm told you can sing."

"No."

"Father McCall thinks so. He said you have promise, a natural talent."

"I don't sing." He ran his hand through his hair, glanced at the ceiling then down at the large shoes on Prentiss's extended feet. In a slow steady voice, he said, "I can't read, I can't write, and I can't sing. You want to know what's in my brain? That's it. I'm not a proper student for your school."

"I see. Well, nothing ventured, nothing gained, a misunderstanding I suppose. Perhaps you're right. You'll need to return the uniform, of course."

Colin didn't know whether to feel relieved or disappointed that they would let him go so easily but wasn't pleased with the idea of giving up his new clothes.

"Son, before you go, can you help me with something? I've a class in here next hour. There are twenty-five students coming for the lesson. It seems I only have seventeen chairs. How many more should I request from storage?"

"Eight." He said, annoyed the subject had changed, wondering if perhaps he should try to stay. He wanted to read, after all, but feared how students would treat him once they knew he couldn't.

"You needn't worry. It's clear you don't want to stay. I'll tell Father he was mistaken. Now, what was I thinking? I just realized three of those students are absent today. How many chairs will I need?"

"Five. Before you say anything to Father McCall, do you ever teach reading to someone who isn't a student? Maybe someone who runs errands for you?"

"So, you've an interest in reading but not in school? I could mention that to the Reverend. I'll also tell him you have a head for mathematics. You add and subtract without thinking. That's a sure sign of true intelligence."

No one ever suggested Colin might be smart. It certainly wasn't anything he thought of himself. He sat straighter.

Their conversation lasted another half hour, ending with agreement that Colin would take three classes. He would learn reading, music, and math, each taught one-on-one until he mastered the basics. Choirmaster Thompson would handle the music, and Prentiss would cover the other lessons. When not in class, he would be in the small, cramped library studying his lessons and improving his skills. Those would be in addition to his religious education, of course. St. Anne's would never ignore the soul.

Colin felt a stiffness ease from his body. He banished tension with a long sigh and replaced it with a faint spark of hope. Perhaps school might be manageable after all. He still wasn't sure about music, and religion frightened him, but if he could learn to read.

He thought about the letter hidden in his mother's biscuit tin under the wharf. He would know what his father wrote.

Prentiss reached long thin fingers into his vest pocket, withdrawing a silver watch on a lengthy chain. He flipped open the case with one hand while pushing his spectacles farther up his nose with the other then peered into the watch face. He snapped it shut, returning it to his pocket with one swift motion.

"I've a class soon. You and I will begin our first lesson immediately after lunch. It's time you learned some letters. Have they given you chores yet?"

"Chores?"

"We all contribute, lad. Do you have an assignment?"

"No, sir. I've not heard."

"We will have to get that sorted out. For now, I'd like you to return to the dormitory and tend each fire, the one in the main room and the one in the bathroom as well. They need a good stoking to burn throughout the morning. Wesley usually handles that, but he's in the infirmary today. Can you handle that?"

"I can."

"Well, there's your first chore. Get to it. Your lesson will be in this room."

Stoking a roaring fire didn't seem so much a chore as a fun thing to do. He climbed back up to the dormitory and set about replenishing each of the fires with thick dry logs. He watched the sparks dance as he placed each piece of wood and felt the flash of warmth as the flames erupted and the logs crackled. Colin brushed his hands briskly back and forth to clear the soot and was about to rub them on the front of his pant legs, but the image of Millicent scolding him intervened, and he rubbed them on a towel instead.

He decided to lie on his cot until lunch and headed in that direction but was distracted by shouts from the courtyard below. From the window, he looked down to see a ring of boys gathered around Blaine and Malcolm. Blaine was taunting the smaller boy and knocked his books to the ground. Colin knew Malcolm as the boy who'd first befriended him yesterday and felt an impulse to rush to his defense.

Before he could move, a tall thin boy dropped to all fours directly behind Malcolm. Blaine smiled and shoved his victim back, sending him tumbling over the boy behind him. A large sloppy student bulging out of his uniform flopped onto Malcolm, pinning him to the grass. Blaine bent down, whispered something in his victim's ear, flicked his finger sharply onto Malcolm's nose three times, then finished with a hard slap. The other students backed away as the bully and his two accomplices headed for the dining hall. Colin didn't know the names of those two yet, but from then on, he thought of them as Weasel and the Ox.

First Lesson

Colin arrived after lunch for his first lesson, intimidated but eager to learn. The room was empty. Prentiss wasn't there. The piano bench was bare, and the gaslights, unlit. He stepped out into the hall, looked up and down the corridor, then cautiously walked back in, fearing it might be a hoax, that no one really intended to teach him anything.

He went to the piano, looking at the black and white keys, studying their pattern, hovering the fingers of his right hand over them, and then striking the white ones with three of his fingers. The notes were louder than he expected. He straightened and stepped back, turning to see if anyone heard him. The room remained dim and silent.

Satisfied he was alone, Colin sat on the bench. He extended the index finger of his left hand and pushed one of the middle keys, then each of its neighbors from left to right and back again. He tried just the black keys next and listened as the sound varied from one stroke to the next. Higher notes, lower notes, mangled discordant notes when he mashed too many keys with all his fingers. He found the floor pedals and played with them to see the difference they made.

Colin placed each index finger on the middle keys, striking them, moving away from each one so the left finger struck lower notes while the right moved into higher tones.

Prentiss stood in the doorway, quietly watching the boy. It was clear his actions were more than idle tinkering. Colin was learning, listening carefully to the notes of each white key, and then each black one. Occasionally, the boy tilted his head sideways, closer to the instrument, repeating a keystroke, striking it until he'd captured its sound.

Prentiss turned up the gas light next to the door. "You've an active mind, son. I suspect you'll master that in no time. First, I'll instruct you on reading, and then I'll show you the language of music."

Colin turned abruptly from the piano as if caught breaking the law.

"The room was empty. I just wanted to hear the sound."

"It's fine, boy. Sorry to be late. There was a scuffle in the courtyard before lunch. A necessary bit of discipline had to be administered. I wonder if you saw what happened?"

"I was tending to the fires, sir."

"Of course. I've some items for you."

He went to a cupboard at the back of the room and brought out a sheaf of lined paper, three pencils, and a rubber gum eraser.

"Do you know the alphabet?"

"Some, sir. Just A, B, C, D."

"Good. This won't be too difficult. First, we'll have you copy the letters, there are twenty-six of them, and then we'll learn their sounds. After that, it's just a matter of putting the pieces together."

He took a primer from the top shelf of the cabinet and opened it, so Colin could see the letters of the alphabet spread across the top of two pages.

"First, we'll recite them. It's quite easy. Then I'll have you copy them onto paper, one full page for 'A,' one for 'B,' etc. Let me see how you hold a pencil."

Colin took hold with a clumsy grasp, but with some guidance, soon took control of it. With that, the first lesson began. Colin was learning to read and write.

Math was next. Colin could add and subtract in his head but didn't know how to express it on paper, and had only a bare understanding of multiplication, even less of division.

Prentiss used a slate blackboard to write simple equations that Colin slowly copied onto paper, keeping his eraser close at hand for frequent use. Bouts of frustration often tempted him to throw his pencil across the room. Each lesson lasted twenty minutes. His patience was wearing thin.

"Your music lessons will begin soon. Let's take a break before Choirmaster Thompson arrives. You've my permission to visit the courtyard or return upstairs for twenty minutes."

Colin trudged up to the dormitory expecting it to be vacant but discovered Malcolm lying on his cot holding a blood-stained handkerchief to his nose. His left eye was swollen, turning purple and black. He'd been crying.

"I saw what Blaine did. Are you all right?"

"My nose won't stop bleeding. I was sent here without lunch. Blaine told them it was my fault, and everyone was too afraid to tell the truth."

"Wait here. I'm going to get you something."

Colin bounded down the stairs, two at a time, turning right at the landing and heading across the courtyard to the kitchen.

He heard dishes being washed and knives chopping vegetables for the evening meal, smelled fish and lemon. His skills of stealth came in handy as he crouched below a counter, waiting for the cook to move one way so he could move the other. Still in a bent position, he quietly duck-walked, keeping below the chopping table until he reached the pantry. Two quick movements yielded cheese and a pear. He was gone with no one knowing he'd been there.

He handed the food to Malcolm. "I saw the fight from up here. Everyone knows it's not your fault. Why doesn't anyone stand up to Blaine?"

"Some have tried. But even if they can best him, Toby and Chester would intervene." Colin would always think of them as Weasel and the Ox.

"I've seen them. They wouldn't last five minutes on their own. If you tame Blaine, those two will fall in line."

Cold Morning

Frigid air streamed through the dormitory on winter nights. Colin had known worse but still found it hard to sleep. He rolled on his side, pulling the blanket tight around him, listening to the slumbering noises of his schoolmates until sleep finally came.

He awoke shivering, keeping the blanket around him as he rose and padded to the trunk at the end of his cot, where he quickly put on his shirt and trousers. Other boys were up, busy with washing and dressing. Colin bent down to grab his shoes and socks from under the bed. He couldn't feel them, so he went down of one knee and peered into gray light underneath. They weren't there. He could tell they weren't but nevertheless extended his arm as far as it would reach and waved it back and forth, thinking he might just be too tired to see them.

A burst of laughter caught his attention. He looked around to see Blaine, Weasel, and Ox standing by the washroom door staring at him. The ringleader smiled with arrogant satisfaction on his face. Weasel gave Ox a good-natured punch on the shoulder and received a menacing look in return. Blaine strode to the top of the stairs, close to the end of Colin's cot.

"Time for prayer boys. Mustn't keep Father waiting. You know the punishment for missing chapel." He looked at Colin and smirked.

The punishment for missing morning prayers was missing the evening meal. A student was sent to bed hungry with the admonition: "If you won't nurture your spirit, we'll not nurture your stomach."

Colin balled his fists and took a step toward Blaine, but Ox blocked his path, and Malcolm grabbed his arm from behind to restrain him. Instead of coming to blows, the boys glared at each other. Blaine mumbled "river rat" under his breath and led the students downstairs. Colin stood alone for a full minute, his fists clenched tight, and then followed the others, barefoot, down the steps out into the courtyard freshly covered in cold wet snow.

As they filed into church, Father McCall spotted the shoeless boy and approached from the altar. Colin was about to slip into a pew with the others when the priest stopped him.

"Where are your shoes, lad?"

Colin looked up at the cleric and then to others. Blaine was in the first pew turning around, giving him a threatening look.

He looked down at his cold wet feet and curled his toes. "I've misplaced them, sir."

"I see," he motioned for Colin to join the others in their pew and walked slowly to the front of the church, where he turned staring at the boys, his stern gaze settling directly on Blaine.

"Well, Colin's come to pray without his shoes. Careless boy! I'm hereby instructing him, with all of your help, to locate his shoes by end of breakfast or they'll be no dinner for any of you tonight." His eyes never left Blaine's.

"Do you understand?"

After prayers, Colin trudged back with the others, trying to step in their footprints rather than into deeper snow. His legs and icy toes quivered under the table throughout breakfast, but he sat defiantly, not giving the slightest indication he was uncomfortable. Eventually, Blaine whispered something to Weasel, who laughed, nodding his head, excused himself, and slinked upstairs.

When the boys headed to class, Colin bounded up the steps to find his footwear sitting in the middle of his cot, his socks stuffed into each shoe. He pulled one out and was greeted with a sharp pungent odor. Three sardines waited under each sock. Colin dumped them into the palm of his hand and took them to Blaine's bed. His was the closest to the large stone fireplace.

Good, Colin thought as he placed them under the pillow, *the heat should rot them nicely.*

Homecoming

Warren Phelps gripped the ship's railing as it sailed into Liverpool. Light rain and wind blew directly in his face as he squinted toward the harbor.

England! Even through the rain and smoke-laden sky, it was a welcome sight. He was filled with excitement and relief. Relief that, after five years, his voyage had finally brought him home when so often he feared he might never see England again, and excitement he would be with Dottie and Colin at last.

He often thought of how she might have reacted when his letter came. It would have taken weeks to arrive. Warren pictured her smiling as she read. She would have sat in their only upholstered chair, reading by the light of the window, twirling a strand of hair with her fingers.

Perhaps she wept a bit with joy, or maybe laughed out loud with delight. She would have raised her dainty hand up to her smiling lips. He imagined her calling Colin over and reading it to him while the boy knelt beside her. He could see her explaining to him what it meant for their future. He thought she might read it again by candlelight at night, falling asleep with it cradled to her chest.

Warren returned on the clipper ship *Sovereign of the Seas*. The ship was known for setting a record for the fastest speed ever recorded by a sailing ship. In 1854, she'd achieved the remarkable pace of twenty-two knots, shattering expectations by sailing from New York to Liverpool in thirteen days, fourteen hours.

He could have paid full fare. He was a man of means now. But her passenger manifest was full, so Warren signed on as crew. He was happy to load cargo, work the riggings, and clean decks. Anything that got him to England faster was fine with him.

As soon as he could leave the ship, he bounded onto the dock and rushed to the purser's office to complete the ship's paperwork and collect his pay, though money was the least of his interests. He rebuffed the advances of prostitutes, asked directions to the train station, then set out, nearly running, with his canvas bag swinging at his side. He needn't have hurried. The train wouldn't arrive for another two hours.

He spent the time talking with passengers, eager to learn all that happened while he was away.

The Crimean War had just ended. Napoleon III had visited London in appreciation for England's partnership in the fight. Queen Victoria and Prince Albert returned the favor with a visit to France.

Victoria had been on the throne for some twenty years, survived three assassination attempts, and recently given birth to her eighth child. The birth was controversial. Her Majesty used a new drug, an anesthetic called chloroform, to ease the pain. The church was outraged she had "violated biblical teaching."

Warren earnestly wanted to know everything that happened while he was away but had difficulty concentrating. His thoughts kept drifting to Dottie and Colin. When the train arrived, he boarded the front car so he'd be among the first to disembark in London.

He made a quick stop at Victoria Station, purchasing flowers for Dottie and a toy soldier for Colin before hailing a cab. Warren grew increasingly anxious by the slow pace of the horse and the heavy traffic that often brought them to a stop.

Despite his frustration he tipped the driver generously when they reached his home. Warren tried the doorknob. It was locked. He banged loudly and could feel his own heart beating with excitement.

The landlord, Julian Blessing, opened the door, then opened his mouth and stared incredulously at Warren.

"Master Phelps! We thought you'd … perished."

"I'm happily quite alive, Mr. Blessing, and eager to see my family."

"Your family … yes, of course. It seems your family, your wife is …"

"Is what?"

The landlord paused. He rubbed the palms of his hands slowly up and down on the front of his trousers. His head bowed down a bit and his shoulders hunched. He raised his eyes to look Warren in the face.

"I find I have the misfortune of informing you your dear wife is lost."

"Lost?"

"To cholera. It's been over a year now. I'd no way to reach you. No one to tell."

The flowers fell from Warren's hand.

"And my son? Where is Colin?"

"Alive. I believe."

"You believe?! Alive where?"

"I … I wouldn't know, sir."

"The hell you don't! Where's Colin?"

"He left when his mother died. I haven't seen him since."

Warren delivered a crushing blow to the landlord's face, knocking him three steps into the lobby, where he collapsed onto his back. Warren grabbed him by the collar with both hands, jerking him into a sitting position.

"You bastard! You threw him out! Where'd he go?"

"Sir, I've no idea …"

"You've no idea what I'll do to you if you don't find him." He pulled Blessing up onto his feet. "You're going to help me find my boy, and you'll move heaven and earth to do it! Do you understand? And what of my belongings? My furniture and possessions?"

The landlord shrugged meekly.

"I sent Dottie a letter ..."

"All gone, I am afraid. We thought you were dead."

Warren slapped him hard and fast across his ear. "You'll be dead, you filthy parasite! Let me be clear about this: you and I will spend every minute of every day looking for my son until we find him."

He paused suddenly, staring intently at the landlord for several seconds, and then extended his arms, placing a hand on each of Blessing's shoulders. "Where is she? Where did they take her?"

"Norwood, sir, like so many others. She was laid to rest in Norwood Cemetery. It was a proper Christian burial, I'm sure."

Warren's frame sank. With his hands still on Blessing's shoulders, he lowered his head almost to the landlord's chest, leaning into him for several seconds. His short shallow breaths were followed by large heaving ones and then the quiet words, "Take me to her."

Norwood

The cemetery, only twenty years old, was on the site of the Great North Wood, from which it took its name. Some of the grand, ancient trees were preserved, but most were gone. From the two stone octagonal towers that flanked the entrance of its consecrated grounds, Warren could see countless stones and markers competing for space. He turned to Blessing for guidance, but the landlord only shrugged.

"So many died in the epidemic, so many since, I've no idea where she lies."

Warren pushed past him to the round stone office, administered by the Diocese of Winchester. A short pudgy man sat at work writing notations in a thick ledger, illuminated by fluttering candlelight, barely looking up as the two men entered. When he did lift his head, his eyes and breath announced he'd been drinking.

His dull gaze rested on Warren as if his request for a burial location was in a foreign language. Warren raised his voice, and the caretaker seemed to come to life.

"Date of death?'

"Her name is Dottie Phelps, Dorothy Phelps!"

"Date of death. That's how we record them, not by names."

Warren turned to Blessing. "When did she die?"

The landlord cocked his head in thought. "I was stricken as well. Almost died myself. Late summer 1854, August, I think."

The caretaker placed his hands flat on the table, bent his arms at the elbows, and pushed himself to a standing position.

"Cholera? Summer of 1854, was it? That was a busy time for us. I've the ledgers nearby."

He waddled to a bookshelf at the far corner of the room, lifting his candle and squinting while pointing his index finger at the books and slowly moving from left to right.

"Ah. Here we are." He carried the thick ledger back to the table and let it fall with a dull thud.

"She'll be in here, I wager." He opened it and lowered his head to the book, nearly touching it with his nose, and again used his pudgy finger to slide down the list of names.

"Phelps, did you say?"

"Phelps! Dorothy!" her husband nearly yelled.

When her name was found, the little man announced the number of her plot and waved his arm, giving slurred directions to its location.

Warren hurried out with the landlord trailing behind, trying to match his pace.

The directions were far from clear, but they found her after several wrong turns. She lay under a modest marker, the temporary kind used for paupers, the kind that would fade and crumble over time.

Warren removed his hat and knelt in front of her grave. He reached out, stroking her marker with his fingers, his head down, eyes closed, praying. His other hand felt the strands of grass growing over her, and he placed his palm where he imagined her heart to be.

"Dottie, my dear sweet Dottie. I've been such a fool. I hope in heaven you know I've thought of you constantly. I only wanted to make you happy. I presumed my actions would assure your happiness. But I was gone too long, filled with too much pride. Dottie, I went to find our fortune and lost the greatest treasure I had in you. It's all so empty now except for Colin. You must know he's lost, but I'll find our boy. I promise you, Dottie, everything I have will be his. I will keep your memory alive in him."

He loosened his tie and collar to reach behind his neck and removed the thin chain and silver cross she had given him for safety on his voyage. Warren placed it gently on her grave and wept while the landlord stood awkwardly by.

When his tears were exhausted, he rose and approached Blessing. "Now you're going to help me find my son!"

And indeed, they looked. They talked to every boy they saw, searched the parks, visited orphanages and hospitals, talked to constables, dock workers, and station masters. They followed every lead. Warren even paid London's bobbies to work overtime on the search. It never occurred to him to inquire at churches.

They came across a crew of lightermen at the docks who said they knew Colin. They'd seen him, talked with him, and shared meals with him.

"Thank God! Do you know where he is now?"

"Afraid not. We ain't seen him in months. He liked to talk about voyages. Always said he wanted to follow you to sea. Said he fancied a trip to the New World."

"Which New World? America or Australia?"

"America, I think."

"Did he ever mention a letter?"

"A letter?"

"I sent his mother a letter. Did he talk of it?"

"Not as I recall. We didn't know he could read." He gestured toward the other crew, who mostly shrugged or shook their heads no.

Their search continued for nine anxious weeks, to no avail. The boy must have left London or perished. There was no other conclusion to draw. Warren's heart sank deeper with every week. The joy he'd felt on arriving in London was replaced by thick, angry, black brooding.

Frequently, an irresistible fury rose within him. Those were the times he came closest to lashing out and violently ending the landlord's life. Always, he stopped just short, knowing two searchers were better than one.

The landlord tried more than once to avoid Warren, to be done with the search. But each time he was made to know his very life depended on his full commitment to finding the boy.

Warren Phelps finally acknowledged the futility of their quest. He allowed Blessing to go back to his landlord chores, but only with a strict promise to notify him of any possible lead.

His business affairs in America needed attention, and his fortune needed protection, though his heart wasn't in his wealth anymore. It felt hollow and useless without Dottie and Colin. He came to despise it. If he had stayed in London, he'd be poor as a church mouse but rich in family and love. Now all that was gone.

Nevertheless, he had responsibilities, and serious practical reasons for attending to his business interests. He also harbored a faint hope Colin might have read his letter and left for America to find him.

Warren visited the office of George Covington, a well-known barrister at Westminster Hall. The Honorable Mister Covington practiced exclusively at the King's Bench, representing a most distinguished clientele. Covington was instructed to create a trust for Colin.

Perhaps the boy was irretrievably lost, unlikely to ever appear. But if he did, the Bank of England would transfer 500 pounds into an account on his behalf. George Covington, or his designee, would supervise the money for Colin until his eighteenth year, and Warren Phelps would be notified, by the fastest possible conveyance, of the boy's location.

That precise sum was deposited in an account with the bank, to earn interest at four percent, from which the institution would draw its annual administrative fee. If the boy were not located after ten years, the money would revert to an account in the sole name of Warren Phelps.

With the arrangement completed, Warren asked Covington: "Can I rely on your complete discretion? I've another request to make. It must be completely secret, not just with you but with any successors who might follow you."

"Discretion carries to every member of our firm. Any contracts you make with me, or my successors, will be held in the utmost confidence."

Warren studied him for several seconds. "Very well. I've another responsibility for you. It involves a sum to be paid each year. I will deposit 1,000 pounds annually to be paid to Mrs. Amanda Winters of 1047 Abington Trace. The payments are to be purely anonymous. If anyone ever learns the source of these payments, you will face immediate and severe legal actions."

Covington raised his eyebrows and leaned back on his chair, pondering the implications. "You can count on us to be discreet. No one will discover the source of those payments."

Taking Charge

Colin finished his sixth month at St. Anne's just as his father abandoned the search. In his mind, he still had one foot out the door. But the food was good, most of the boys were friendly, and there were still things he wanted to learn about this place, and these people, before striking out again. More than anything, he wanted to continue his reading lessons.

His problems with Blaine were resolved eleven days after he arrived. Saturday mornings were mostly free time. Choir practice wouldn't begin until two in the afternoon, so the boys could play football matches on the green, shoot marbles, or wander to nearby shops, though most had few, if any, coins.

Colin still appreciated the comfort of being in a safe room and having his own cot and pillow. He was sound asleep when Blaine crept up beside him. He'd been eyeing the gold ring on the leather strip around Colin's neck. His knife was small, the blade not more than two inches long. He paused a minute, studying Colin's breathing pattern. The cut should be quick, but the real challenge was to deftly lift both the leather strip and ring without waking his victim.

He reached down, gently pinching a bit of leather with his left hand, slipping the knife under with his right, and using his right thumb to crimp the leather tight while he made a quick upward slice. He smiled as it came free. All he needed was to gently slide the ring off without waking Colin.

Colin's right hand flashed, grabbing Blaine's ear in a tight twisting grip. He yanked Blaine's head down to his own chest, pinning him there. Blaine squirmed, readying his knife to strike Colin's thigh. Before he could make the thrust, Colin's other hand slammed into his nose. The knife fell as Blaine tried to rear his head up, but his ear was still squeezed firmly in his victim's fingers.

The next attack from Colin was subtle, but far more effective. His fingers pressed against Blaine's eyes, pushing firmly until the boy screamed for mercy. Colin gave the ear another firm twist and then yanked it straight up, sending Blaine over backwards onto the floor.

The ring fell between the cot and Blaine. Colin leapt to his feet, then smashed both his knees on top of Blaine's chest, leaving him breathless. As Blaine gasped for air, Colin picked the ring up and held it over Blaine's face.

"You will never touch me or anything of mine again! Do you understand?"

Blaine blinked, trying to urge air into his lungs.

"In fact, you won't hurt any of the boys here! Is that clear?"

Blaine nodded slowly waving his arm above him in an "I'm done" motion.

Colin threaded the leather strap through his mother's ring, standing over Blaine, glaring at him, while he tied the length around his neck.

No one witnessed the fight, but they soon recognized its aftermath. Blaine was deferential to Colin. That night when the dinner bell rang, Blaine started to take his place at the front of the others, but Colin shot him a look, and he stood aside. He waited for his proper place in line. At dinner, he let the other boys take their helpings in turn and took only what he needed.

A Sad Departure

Warren Phelps looked up at the ship that would take him back to America. He cinched his raincoat tight around him, one hand clutching his suitcase, the other holding the rim of his hat, securing it against the wind and drizzling rain. Leaving England, alone, was the last thing he'd imagined doing when he sailed into Liverpool.

He had come to hate ships. They were his bright and shining promise once, his chance to make something of himself, to rescue his family from desperate, pervasive poverty in a city that relentlessly crushed its poor.

Ships had been his ticket to a new life for his family. London bustled with newfound wealth and promising tales of people who'd found comfort and fortunes in America. Merchants who financed ships, traders who opened new markets, bankers, even heroes of naval escapades in western waters flaunted their success. To hear the stories, America was a land of endless possibility where anyone could prosper.

Five years ago, he had promised Dottie his trip would change their lot. He would find a bright new future and use money wisely to provide a secure life for her and young Colin. Warren kissed her goodbye at the Waterloo dock and nearly bounded up the gangplank, turning to wave and blow kisses from his grinning lips. She held their child secure against her with her left hand while her right waved a linen handkerchief she would soon use to dry her eyes.

Warren realized his son was missing one of his blue woolen mittens. He remembered Colin had dropped it, and he picked it up but got caught in a long loving last embrace with Dottie and absently slipped the mitten into his own pocket. He treasured that last picture of his wife and son in his mind and had revisited it over and over during his absence.

Now he slogged slowly, methodically up the gangplank like a condemned prisoner approaching the gallows. He turned once and looked at the spot where Dottie once stood with their boy. The memory was too painful; he looked away, staring at his boots as he climbed.

His first voyage seemed a lifetime ago. He had secured work as crew on a ship carrying immigrants and all manner of goods to America to be exchanged for cotton, tobacco, furs, corn, and sugar. Warren worked several jobs onboard: he loaded cargo, manned riggings, cleaned crew quarters, and helped prepare meals under a demanding, sadistic cook. Every waking minute was taken up by labor. But he bore it well, knowing the passing days brought him closer to America. He would do anything to create a better life for Dottie and Colin.

His hard work and friendly spirit drew the attention of Captain Zachary Winters, who came to rely on Phelps for more responsible duties.

When they finally arrived in New York, Warren marveled at the energy of the place. It bustled with all manner of humanity.

In the previous ten years, two million immigrants had arrived and now comprised a quarter of New York's population. Irish, Germans, Swedes, Italians, and Poles came seeking new lives. The city's population nearly doubled every seven years during the first half of the 1800s. Immigrants at the dock competed for business with free blacks, often fighting for territory on the docks.

The ship's cargo was unloaded, and trading of goods began, but commerce didn't go as planned. The captain was disappointed by the price his goods commanded. Too many ships were making the same voyage, engaging in the same trade. Most European countries were supplying America's east coast. The west coast was now trading with China. Domestic manufacturers were turning out clothing, furniture, pottery, and machinery. Railroads were opening vast new markets and bringing rich natural resources to American factories. In short, there was less demand and far less money for the cargo sold on Warren's ship. Furthermore, the cost of goods had risen sharply for items they planned to purchase for sale in England.

Costs were so high and proceeds so meager, the captain feared he'd face financial ruin. He withheld a full third of his cargo, deciding to sail south. Surely there'd be more demand in Savannah, and he could acquire cotton there at a fraction of the New York price. He took on items likely to attract buyers in southern states as well as the usual fare for sale in London.

Temptation to stay in New York clawed at Warren. But a sense of obligation, with two years remaining on his contract, and the chance to see more of America kept him onboard. The sail was uneventful. Without her immigrants, the ship seemed nearly empty. Warren enjoyed rare idle time to record his thoughts in the leather journal he kept. He hoped to share every detail with Dottie on his return home.

His first impression of hot, humid Savannah was that he'd landed in Africa. Its docks teamed with Africans, mostly shirtless, mostly burdened with heavy loads, and mostly showing scars across their face or backs. Slavery was more than a way of life: it was the core of southern commerce and economy.

An Auction of People

Their third day ashore proved a turning point in the life of Warren Phelps. He and Captain Winters finished a meal at their boarding house and were walking to the ship when they came across a crowd gathered outside the main warehouse of the port.

Working their way to the front, they realized a slave auction was in progress. Fifteen Africans, of all ages, were chained together facing the crowd. An auctioneer highlighted their merits, pointing out the strength of the bare-chested men, lifting the burlap dresses of the women to show their legs. One girl, perhaps twelve years of age, was heralded as having "years of comfort to provide any southern gentleman."

The buyers laughed, and a raucous bidding war erupted. It was clear the girl's mother was with her, but she was of no interest to the crowd. She cringed and cried as her daughter was bargained for. The high bidder was a large pot-bellied man in his late fifties, smelling of sweat and tobacco, with blotchy red skin and a rough beard. He slapped his leg, let out a joyous yelp, and ambled forward to claim his prize as the girl shrank back in fear and her mother reached out but couldn't quite grasp her. The man lifted the girl under his arm like a sack of grain, grinning and accepting congratulations from his friends.

Later, another line of eight slaves was ushered in front of the crowd, seven men and a thin old woman, hunched at the shoulders, stumbling, nearly falling as the foreman pushed them all forward.

The crowd murmured comments, some appreciating the quality of the Negroes, some laughing at the frail old woman.

A tall, bow-legged farmer in dirty blue overalls approached the line, striding to the front of the tallest slave. "Well now, here's an impressive beast." He felt the man's arms, examined his eyes, and pushed on his stomach searching for abdominal pains. Satisfied, he extended the first two fingers of his right hand, held them horizontally under the slave's nose, then pressed hard with an upward motion forcing the Negro's head back while the thumb of his left hand grasped his chin, yanking his mouth open.

He looked sideways at the auctioneer. "Got two teeth missing on his left side."

"Well, you look closely. There's no infection. He's healthy as an ox."

"Fine. I'll give you $1,200."

The auctioneer waved him off. "You'll stand back and bid with everyone else."

The sale brought high prices. Captain Winters watched closely, impressed at the amount each slave commanded. They were more valuable than most items in his cargo. He calculated the total as sales mounted, wishing he owned Africans to sell.

It had been illegal to bring slaves into the country since a congressional act signed by Thomas Jefferson in 1807. Britain banned the practice even earlier and was enforcing the ban, patrolling the waters between Africa and America. Slave traders on the high seas were captured and charged as pirates, and thousands of Africans were freed.

As a consequence, the indigenous population of American slaves grew increasingly valuable. When the auction was over, Captain Winters approached the auctioneer and offered to buy him a few pints in exchange for some information on the commerce of slaves.

He learned prices, places of sale, customs, features that brought the highest bids, and how to arrange an auction. He confirmed the appetite for Africans was quite robust and should he happen to procure some, the auctioneer would be happy to be of service.

Winters grew excited at the prospects. He stood with a flourish, vigorously shook the man's hand, thanked him for his time, and hurried back to his ship.

Warren had sat quietly next to the captain during the conversation, wondering what the man had in mind since they hadn't any slaves and certainly no legal way of procuring them.

It became clear over the next few days as the captain sold off his cargo, some for prices below market value. Emptying the ship seemed to be his only goal. With the holds nearly bare, he ordered the crew to prepare for a voyage to Cuba.

Cuban Trade

Cuba didn't have restrictions on the importation of slaves, so smugglers who braved the dangers of eluding capture by the English Navy did a good business in Havana. So good, in fact, its population of Africans was outstripping demand. Winters planned to buy as many as he could and then slip them into Savannah or Charleston, where a handsome profit was assured. It helped that the Crimean War pressed most of Britain's naval ships into service far from the Caribbean, reducing their chances of being caught.

Warren felt the warmth of the Caribbean wind and marveled at the white beaches and palm trees of an island land so different from England. The humidity that stifled him in Savannah floated off on sea breezes. He yearned for Dottie and Colin to share this with him. *Someday*, he thought.

Auctions were held twice a month in Havana, far too slow a schedule to satisfy the plans Captain Winters had in mind. He needed a quicker pace. His navigator spoke Spanish and was enlisted to negotiate a solution. As suspected, the solution was money. The right bribes would allow him access to slaves before the auction took place. His goal was sixty Africans. Since some might perish on the trip, he settled on seventy-five as the optimal number.

He bought them in a series of night meetings at a large tobacco barn outside the city. Slaves were chained and marched behind a long, horse-drawn wagon. Their merchant sat on the buckboard with a guard holding a shotgun on his right while armed men on horseback guarded the back of the procession.

Some slaves were newly arrived in Cuba, while others had been purchased, or perhaps kidnapped, from plantations farther inland. Winters preferred the latter. They were accustomed to work, while the new arrivals were too frightened and in need of more acclimation to be any good. Still, they would bring a good price.

Over the next three weeks he built a sizable stable of goods. He needed to warehouse them in another barn under the watchful eye of armed members of his crew. As the numbers grew, his crew became more and more apprehensive, feeling pressure to assert authority to intimidate their chattel. When the time came, their cargo would be brought to the ship in small groups, after two o'clock in the morning.

Warren stayed on the ship with some of the crew, outfitting her for the next voyage and guarding her remaining freight. The captain stayed with the men holding his slaves. One of the crew returned to the ship with a story that Captain Winters was selecting a different young girl each night to "amuse himself."

On the day before the slaves were to be taken to the ship, Warren was driven to the site to help oversee the transfers. He arrived to find one of his mates holding a shovel and wiping sweat from his brow. Warren realized the man was standing aside a freshly dug grave. He peered down to see the body of a small black girl, likely not more than twelve years old, scrunched and folded into a pit too short to hold her. He was told the captain amused himself a bit too much last night. Warren turned away and vomited.

This is not what I signed up for when I left Dottie and Colin for a new life. He heaved again, placing his hands on his knees, breathing hard, with sweat beading from his face and anger building from deep within.

A sudden sharp force drove him to the ground as the captain's boot crashed into the middle of his back. He fell onto his own vomit.

"Are you feel'n' ill, Phelps? I hope you're not developing feelings for these monkeys." Winters grabbed him by the back of his shirt with both hands, lifting and turning him onto his back.

"You've got to show 'em who's in charge, instill fear in 'em, make them respect us. This cargo means chink for you, Phelps! More money than you signed on for, and enough money to get that family of yours out of poverty."

Warren looked at him, a white rage building deep inside. He tried to get up, but Winters put his boot on his chest, forcing him back to the ground.

"You get 'em loaded onto the ship, we make one short sail, and these slaves will fetch enough money to brighten all our futures. If you're not man enough for this, tell me now and I'll end your contract right here." He brandished a long gutting knife. "Are you on my crew or not?"

Warren's chest heaved. He stared up at Winters for a long moment and then spread his arms wide, indicating surrender.

"You're the captain," was all he said.

Winters slowly eased his foot from Warren's chest.

"Get them on board, all of 'em. We can't afford to lose a single one. Do we have an understanding?"

Phelps gave a subtle nod. Winters reached down, taking him by the arm and lifting him to his feet.

"Get cleaned up and get 'em to the ship."

Their cargo was loaded under cover of darkness while the ship was made ready for a speedy departure.

With his slaves secured below, and the ship safely out of Havana harbor, Captain Winters sought Warren out. He carried a bottle of rum and two tall pewter mugs; pouring each tankard nearly to the rim, he handed one to Phelps.

"I know I went a bit too far back there. But you'll feel better when your pockets are bulging, and your finances are stable. Let's agree to let bygones be bygones and embrace a better future." He hoisted his mug. Warren gradually raised his and clinked it against the captain's.

"To a better future. Walk with me." He led Warren back to his cabin, where he sat behind a mahogany desk.

"It's our destiny, you and me; we're not ordinary men! We hold our fate in our hands and have only to take what's ours." He filled each mug as soon as they were empty and grinned with yellow crooked teeth. "I like you, Phelps; you and I can take hold of our destinies together."

When the bottle was empty, the captain staggered to a cabinet next to his bed and pulled out another bottle. "Cuba's finest," he smiled, slumping back into his chair. He filled the mugs, singing, "Heavy the seas that will challenge a man, strong is the man who can challenge the sea," and chuckled to himself.

"You know," he said, raising his eyebrows and grinning, "you should try one of them. They can give a man a certain amount of pleasure." The captain's hand bumped the tankard, spilling rum across his desk. "Yes. There's pleasure to be had." His head lolled forward and fell onto his arms on the desk, passed out.

Warren stood on unsteady feet and placed his hands wide apart on top of each side of the desk, staring down at the drunken skipper. In his mind, he saw the crumpled body of a small African girl. He reached out, grasping the rum bottle by its neck and swinging it high over the captain's head, then paused, breathing hard, his hand shaking. He slowly placed the bottle back on the desk, leaned down, and spat on Winters before returning to his quarters.

Savannah Exchange

When their ship reached Savannah, they anchored far outside the harbor. Only two of her slaves had perished, their bodies thrown overboard. Captain Winters, Warren Phelps, and their navigator rowed to shore in search of the auctioneer.

They found him in a tavern and whispered they had cargo that could use his services. He hushed them, reminding them bringing contraband into Georgia was a crime but hinting he could help. He stressed the danger, emphasizing his services would be costlier. They adjourned to his home for privacy.

The auctioneer balled his fist, extending his index finger, which he used to forcefully tap the table with every word he uttered.

"This is dangerous. There's no paperwork verifying ownership of your cargo. Slaves showing up with no lineage of ownership can create a considerable problem. People ask questions and I can't produce documents, well, it's my head." Pounding his fist on the table, he paused, then slowly smiled. "I can create paperwork. But it's expensive."

"What do you need to make this work?"

"Thirty-three percent of proceeds … no less."

Winters stood abruptly. "That's not even close to fair. I took all the risk, procured the cargo, and transported them here. I'll find someone less selfish."

The auctioneer stood, staring steadily into the captain's eyes. "Good luck. Seventy some slaves show up suddenly for sale. You don't think that'll raise questions? You and your crew are strangers here. I have to live in Savannah. I've a reputation to protect, a reputation I spent years building. Go ahead, find someone else … if you can."

"Twenty percent."

"Listen to me. I sell those Negroes of yours and someone shows up claiming ownership, it's my neck in the ringer. Do you have any idea what it takes to produce bills of sale for so many slaves? It's too dangerous."

The captain placed the palm of his hand on the auctioneer's chest, grabbing his shirt and pulling him in. "They're from Cuba. No one's coming for them."

"Great! Am I supposed to say they came from Virginia or the Carolinas when not one of them speaks a word of English? I'll wager half of them have been branded. It's not a risk worth taking."

He motioned them toward the door.

Winters winced, folded his arms across his chest, and said, "Thirty-three percent for so many slaves is too dear."

"Fine. Twenty-five percent. I'm taking all the risk, and you're taking seventy-five percent of the profit."

Taking the measure of the auctioneer, the captain slowly unfolded his arms. He extended his right hand. "Done!"

With the deal struck, they agreed to unload the slaves fifteen miles up the coast at a private cove, where the auctioneer would meet them and transport the goods to a secluded farm so they could be evaluated before sale.

The results exceeded Captain Winter's every dream. He rejoiced at the price each African commanded. Rather than sell all of them at once, five auctions were held, ten days apart: all commanded top dollar.

Afterwards, the captain sat alone at the trader's home where the proceeds were exchanged for gold coins, which the captain counted several times before locking them securely in his personal chest.

Captain Winters insisted they celebrate their success with fine Cuban rum, moderating his own intake, while waiting patiently, drink after drink, for the liquor to do its work. The broker wobbled in his chair, then laid his head down on his chest. Winters drew a blade from his belt, two quick thrusts and the auctioneer's share of the treasure was now his as well.

Captain Winters watched carefully as the bounty was escorted to his ship under armed guard, then hastened his crew to make sail right away.

Back on board and under way, he paced the ship like an emperor surveying his kingdom, rubbing his hands together, delighting in how his fortunes had changed, planning how to spend his way into a solid, upper-class life. He almost skipped. Maybe he would make this voyage again, repeating the transaction to multiply his wealth.

He'd need a new auctioneer, of course.

Cold air rushed up, blowing his thin hair back as he stood on deck, hardly noticing the rising waves and the dark clouds building on the horizon.

His sailors grew apprehensive, urging a return to Savannah, but the captain insisted they keep the sails taut and race it out. They were headed north, hugging the shoreline. He wanted some distance, hoping to outrun the storm and at least make the port of Baltimore, still planning to make New York where certain items held a special appeal to him.

For the next five hours, it seemed they would make it. Heavy winds brought pounding rain and high seas, but they gradually abated. Winters embraced the calm as another sign he was destined to succeed where others failed. He pitied the average man who would wilt at the first signs of trouble.

Waves relaxed as the wind subsided and the rain settled into little more than a mist. The relieved crew tightened her sails, pulling for speed. Even seagulls were back in flight.

Warren walked the ship, examining her for signs of damage, making sure she'd withstand another battering. He reported that all appeared secure but cautioned the captain they should seek shore until all was clear.

"You underestimate me, Mr. Phelps. I've been through far worse storms, seen more than you can imagine. Our course is due north, and your task is to make up for lost time."

Warren wanted to speak but sighed and returned to his station.

Reaching Shore

They were off the coast of North Carolina across from the Outer Banks near Hatteras in the dead of night when the wind changed, and rain pelted them in heavy sheets. Waves rose, sending the ship into frighteningly high rocking motions, rapidly intensifying, pitching the ship higher, slamming it violently down into the ocean, shuddering as waves crested and rushed over her deck. The wind raged and howled like a wounded beast. Captain Winters capitulated, screaming to his crew to salvage the ship, pointing through the rain toward the shore. "Make for land!"

The crew searched for refuge, turning port side in a desperate effort to outrun the storm. They fought the elements for nearly an hour, steadily losing hope until the faint distant flash of a lighthouse pierced the rain and darkness.

Land was in sight, sparking new courage. Muscles strained as sailors made every attempt to hold their course. Blue-white lightning stabbed the sky as the ship rose forty-five degrees under an enormous wave, then dropped rapidly, engulfed in water. Two of her crew fell overboard, unnoticed. Deckhands pleaded for land, prayed to make shore, just as their ship hit a reef with a sharp shattering sound and split apart.

Panic erupted, with sailors rushing to the lifeboats. Captain Winters strained against the wind and sheeting rain, his body bent, using a rope line to steady him as he moved methodically to his cabin.

He lifted the heavy lockbox from under his bed and cradled it with both arms, pushing against the cabin door with his hip and staggering back on deck. He made it to the closest lifeboat, where Warren was already directing others aboard. The captain pushed a sailor aside; the man slid onto his back and slipped away with the steep list of the ship.

Warren and another sailor made it into the little boat when the captain bulled his way on and loosened the rope, sending it rapidly into the water. The force of the impact nearly bounced its passengers overboard. Warren steadied himself, stretching his arms to grab each side of the boat. He looked up to see members of the crew gaping down at them in horror. Some of the other boats were set free, but many of the crew were left helpless on deck.

Captain Winters held the treasure chest firmly against his body while Warren and the other sailor, Bennett Wilson, grabbed the oars.

"Row! Damn it, row!" the captain screamed above the howling wind. And they did row, heading for land as their tiny boat rose and crashed with every wave, filling with water at an alarming rate. Winters took one arm off his treasure, furtively scooping seawater out with his hat.

"Get me to shore, damn it! I'll pay you handsomely. Just get me to shore!"

Warren and Bennett pulled with all their strength, making progress, approaching land. Waves pushed them closer toward the beach. Bennett laughed and shouted, "We made it! Captain, we made it. We'll gladly take that reward you promised us."

Winters looked alarmed. He kicked Bennett squarely in the chest, knocking the wind out of him, sending him backwards into the roiling water. Ten yards closer, nearly to shore, the captain climbed over the side holding his treasure chest above him, his feet barely touching the sand beneath the waves. He staggered toward the beach until the cresting surf slammed him from behind and he fell under the water.

Warren leapt from the boat to help him. He pulled the captain up out of the tide, but Winters was frantic at having lost his strongbox. He flailed free from Warren and screamed, "My chest! Get my gold!"

Phelps ducked under the waves, feeling left and right but finding nothing. He tried again with no luck, but on his third try his leg brushed against it and he managed to pull it up. He was bent over, exhausted, breathing heavily.

Winters beckoned with both hands for Warren to hand it to him.

"Get ashore first!" Phelps said, trying to catch his breath.

The captain lunged at him, grabbing to pry it from Warren's arms. Warren held it tightly and urged the captain toward the beach, but Winters wouldn't relent. He pulled a knife from his waist, raising it to strike Warren's neck.

Warren moved aside, slipping into the waves. The captain fell forward but quickly found his feet and raised the knife again. Phelps dropped the trunk, blocked the attack, and wrestled the blade from Winters. The captain locked his hands around Warren's throat, applying pressure until the life was nearly drawn from him.

Warren plunged the blade into his assailant's stomach and wrenched it upward with one violent jerk. The captain's eyes went wide, his body stiffened, his hands reached out, gripping Warren by the sleeves of his shirt. Warren was shocked to have stabbed him. He supported the captain, intent on getting him to shore. They had barely taken two steps before Winters stopped. His weight was too much for Warren, he struggled to keep the man upright. The captain stopped breathing, went limp, and slipped below the waves.

Phelps stepped back, losing his balance, nearly falling under the cold water himself. He stood for a minute in the pelting rain, his chest heaving while his heart pounded as if to burst. He was moving toward the beach when his foot hit a heavy object. Reaching down, he felt the outline of the wooden trunk and lifted it from the ocean floor.

Church bells began ringing rapidly from on shore. The lighthouse keeper had discovered the shipwreck, and townspeople were rushing to the sea in full rescue mode. They manned boats, rowing out to find survivors and, perhaps, to discover some valuable cargo.

Sanctuary

WARREN was in shock, standing stock-still in waves up to his belt, watching townspeople streaming toward the water. He clutched the chest close to him and slowly trudged to the beach.

No one noticed him. The current had taken their lifeboat more than three hundred yards south of the dying ship. All attention was focused on the floundering wreckage offshore. He was dazed, trudging up the beach to the nearest street of the little town. A church at the middle of the village had its doors open and lights streaming from inside. It would serve as the haven and hospital for any sailors who could be saved.

He walked sluggishly up its stairs and entered with a sense of grief and reverence. Its only occupant was an elderly priest who knelt at the altar praying for victims at sea.

Warren moved silently into the back pew, looked up at the cross hanging above the altar, placed the chest next to him, and knelt on the narrow prayer cushion. Seawater dripped from his clothes as he shivered uncontrollably and silently prayed for mercy, pleading desperately for forgiveness, pledging his life to the service of others.

"Heavenly Father, I beg you, please. Grant me forgiveness. I never meant to do this; I don't know how I could've taken a life. Guide me, Jesus. Show me what I can do. I'll serve you, Lord! I beg You: give me a chance to follow you, to overcome the wrong I've done. Let me, please, return to my family and live as you would have me do."

The priest felt his presence and left the altar to join him, standing above Warren at the end of the pew.

"Were you on the ship, son?"

Warren flinched at the cleric's words and instinctively put his right arm over the wooden chest.

"Did you survive the storm?"

Warren nodded slowly, his eyes staring at the crucifix over the alter. The priest slid into the pew next to him.

"It must have been an awful trial. Would you like me to pray for you?"

Warren looked at the priest, eyes welling with tears, and mumbled, "I'm a sinner, Father."

"Then you need absolution, my son." The priest placed his arm across Warren's back and prayed for healing, giving thanks he had survived.

When his prayers were done, he turned to Phelps.

"I'm Father Lewis. You'll need a room for the night. You're cold and in shock. We'll be bringing others here. Some will have perished. Are you strong enough to help us identify the bodies of those who are lost?"

Warren felt panic building. He realized Bennett Wilson might have witnessed his fight with Winters, knew others might have seen him leave the ship with the captain and his treasure.

He turned and reached with both his hands to grip the priest's hands in his own.

"I've seen things a man shouldn't have to see, done things I never wanted to do. Are you truly a man of God, Father? Can I rely on you?"

"I'm here only to serve. How may I help you?"

Warren shifted the wet chest onto his lap and then moved it to the priest's side.

"Can you hold this for me? Hold it in sacred trust and not let anyone else know it's here. This is my only worldly possession. Can I entrust it to your care?"

"You have my word."

"People may come looking for it, trying to wrest it from me. It's my life's savings. You must keep it sacrosanct, anyone searching for it will be doing the devil's work. Will you protect it for me?

"You have my bond, but it's not your belongings I care about. Are you a Christian, a believer in our Savior?"

"I am, Father, more than ever in my life."

"Your holdings are safe with me. Come. I'll give you a place to stay. You'll be wanted in the morning to help survivors and identify those who have passed."

He led Warren to his rectory next to the church, where an upstairs guest room was always available to someone in need. The priest carried the lockbox up with him. Phelps gestured to it. "Keep that safe for me, Father. Hide it until I come to you for it."

"It remains in my care, and your salvation remains in my prayers."

"My salvation may rest entirely with this chest, Father. I'm in your hands."

"Then rest assured your redemption is safe. I only hope you aren't storing up salvation on worldly goods. Dry your clothes and get a good night's sleep. I'll send up fresh garments and some supper. This will be a long night, I fear, and you'll be needed at dawn."

Images

It *was* a long night. Nine survivors were rescued, but twelve bodies were washed up on the beach or recovered from the sea. Survivors were split among townsfolk who opened their homes, while the bodies of the dead were laid out in the church. Warren would learn from the count that eleven of his mates were missing, probably forever.

At daybreak the priest came to Warren's room, rousing him for the solemn duty of identifying those who perished.

He entered the church trembling with apprehension, dreading the sight of his comrades lying still and cold on the stone floor, fearing he would be discovered for a murder he never meant to commit.

A tall, weathered man, introducing himself as the mayor, asked Warren to take his time identifying each corpse. Most he knew by name, but some were only vaguely familiar. If he had a manifest listing the crew, he could likely identify each one. Two of the men he knew only by nicknames, and a few were so bloated, and so unfamiliar to him, he couldn't recognize them.

He was nearly finished confirming the identities of the others when three men entered the church carrying the body of a final sailor. This one he could identify immediately. It was Captain Zachary Winters.

An opening in the body's abdomen was clearly visible through his clothes, with a large smear of blood staining down his entire front.

Warren froze, looking around, his chest tight in panic, but he quickly realized only the townspeople were in the church. With the survivors having been housed elsewhere, there was no one to recognize him or the captain.

"This one's been in a fight," one bearer said as they carried his body to the front.

"Please, don't put him near the altar," the priest implored. "Put him on that pew. We can't have him soiling God's holy place."

They obliged, placing him reverently onto the pew halfway up the aisle.

"You know this one?" the cleric asked.

Warren approached the body slowly, feeling queasy, his knees nearly giving out from under him.

His throat became instantly dry, and perspiration beaded on his forehead.

"This was our captain, Zachary Winters. A fine man and a noble leader," he said quietly, almost in a trance. He felt light-headed and sank into the pew directly behind the body.

"He's the last we've found," a man announced. "There may be more, and they may still wash up, but if we haven't recovered them yet, I'm afraid they're lost forever."

Warren knelt on the thin prayer cushion, bent forward, resting his head in his hands on the top of the pew, his eyes closed. He prayed silently that he could find forgiveness, that he would see Dottie and Colin again.

A sudden thought occurred to him: he didn't know if the captain had a family. Would there be a wife and children awaiting his return? Would they someday know Warren had taken his life?

When he opened his eyes, he was staring directly down at the lifeless form of Zachary Winters. He was about to turn away when he noticed a ring of keys hooked around the captain's belt.

"May I have a moment more to pray over my captain?" he asked the priest.

"Of course, son. We'll give you your privacy."

The townspeople turned their attention to those closer to the altar while Father Lewis led them in prayer. With their attention diverted, Warren bent over the body and quietly lifted the keys from the captain's hip.

After prayers, people milled around, discussing the wreck, and wondering about her cargo. Several shook hands with Warren, offering their condolences and help. He was impatient to get away, wondering about Bennett Wilson.

Wilson had been in the rowboat with them and might have seen him fighting with Captain Winters. He wasn't among the bodies brought into the church. Perhaps he'd found shelter in one of the local homes. Perhaps he'd drowned. Warren wasn't sure what fate he hoped for him.

He worked his way to the rear of the church, thanking people for their concern, until he could make a graceful exit and return to the rectory.

Back in his room, he lay on the bed, his fingers pressed firmly on the keys, waiting for sounds to indicate the priest had returned. At mid-day, a woman tapped on his door. She held a wooden tray with bread, cheese, fruit, and tea.

"Father asked that I bring this to you. Is there anything more we can do?'

Warren took the tray, smiled faintly at her, and shook his head as he whispered, "No."

She returned at six o'clock with a large bowl of fish chowder and slices of cornbread.

It was after eight o'clock when the cleric returned. Warren went to his room and knocked on the priest's door.

"Has anyone else been found, Father?"

"I'm afraid the sea has given up all she has. We're not likely to recover any others."

"You've all worked so hard, been so kind. With a storm that violent, it's a miracle you recovered any of us at all. May I have a few minutes with my lockbox?"

The priest looked into the tired, pleading eyes of his rescued sailor. "It's your possession, only in my care as you long as you direct."

"Thank you, Father. I just need a few minutes."

The priest held his door open, pointing to the lockbox on his meager desk before exiting the room. Warren closed the door behind him, went to the chest, and tried each key until he found one that opened the box. As he expected, a large quantity of gold coins filled the box.

What he hadn't expected was a letter, held in a leather case on top, addressed to the captain. He brought the letter closer to the light. It was from Amanda Winters, affirming her love for her husband and advising him of the developments of their three children.

She wrote of her high hopes for the captain's voyage, how anxious she and the children were for his return, eager to know he'd succeeded, that his voyage would earn enough to allow him years on shore with them.

Warren read the letter twice more, crumpled it, and then carefully unfolded it. He looked up to make sure he was alone and placed it back in its pouch, pushing it to the bottom of the coins. He scooped a few of the gold pieces into his pocket and locked the box again.

Warren opened the door and invited Father Lewis back in.

"I commend this back to your care. My life is tied to this; yours may be, too. I beg you, as a man of God, to protect this for me until I return. Will you pray for me, Father?"

They knelt beside the priest's bed while he prayed earnestly for safety and protection of this lost sailor.

Warren's mind raced. He was in a new country and didn't know the people or the geography. With his ship gone he had no employment; he'd not been paid for his services, so his only currency was in the form of gold, and he might well be discovered as a murderer at any moment. He would leave most of the treasure with the priest until he could formulate a plan.

Warren thanked Father Lewis for his kindness, shaking his hand while his other hand rested on the priest's arm.

"I will prove worthy of your prayers, Father."

Back in his room, he slumped onto the bed and fingered the few gold coins in his pockets. Images appeared to him: the girl in her grave, the captain bragging of his prowess, the line of slaves pushed onto the ship, the raging storm, the stunned eyes of Zachary Winters just before he sank below the water.

He remembered four slaves in particular. They appeared to be a family. A father chained to his wife, who in turn was chained to their son and daughter. He saw fear in the parents' eyes, but mostly he saw the boy, a child not much older than Colin. He wasn't downcast like the others but stared defiantly at Warren and the crew, his back straight and his head held high. All were branded, each with a star burned into their left shoulder. Someone had claimed them before, and now they were subject to the whims of Captain Winters and his crew.

Warren felt stung by the boy's glare. He thought of his son and wanted to do something reassuring to give the family hope.

But, instead, he turned away, flushed with guilt, defeated by the dominance of a little boy, images to haunt him the rest of his life.

He turned his thoughts to Dottie and Colin. The captain's treasure was a lifeline for them. He would use it wisely, establish himself, and reclaim his family. And then he thought of Bennett Wilson again. Did he witness Warren plunging the knife into the captain, and did he know the full receipts of their slave trade rested in the chest Warren now possessed?

He undressed and collapsed on to his bed, cradling the modest pillow close to his body, imagining he was holding Dottie, urging himself to sleep.

Sleep came in fits and starts. Too many memories pierced his dreams. He was up before sunlight, pacing his room, trying desperately to plan his future.

Father Lewis knocked on his door at six o'clock, bringing hard-boiled eggs and tea with toast, announcing the survivors would soon be gathered in the church. A service would be held for them, and transport would be arranged; most likely a ship would carry them to Philadelphia or Baltimore where they could find passage back to England.

The Mainland

"Father, I'm ill, too sick to leave my room."

"Of course, Mr. Phelps. How can I help?"

"I need some days to recover my health and no idea how long that may take. I will need quiet and contemplation to seek the Lord. I can pay you for my stay. Can you grant me solitude and time to pray?"

Father Lewis paused. "As I've said, this is your sanctuary. You may stay until you're ready. I'll let the others know your decision."

Warren sat up in bed, raising his hand in a stop gesture. "Please, Father, if they know I'm here, they'll insist I go with them. I'm too weak, and after so much tragedy, I need time alone with God. Can you understand?"

The priest surveyed Warren for several long seconds. "You may have your time with the Lord. We'll be starting the service for your comrades soon if you've the strength for it. If there's something you need to answer for to your fellow sailors, you may want to address it here today."

"It's not that, Father. I feel too fragile to travel and want to start my next journey with Jesus at my side."

"Very well. The room is yours as long as necessary. I'll check on you at midday."

Warren remained secreted in his little room until all his shipmates left. No one came for him; no one reported anything to Father Lewis of a murder or a missing treasure.

He planned to leave a few days later, before anyone returned looking for him. Knowing he was in the clear at least for now, he felt secure taking the chest back. At his request, Father Lewis provided a map of the east coast, and Warren settled on taking a train north until he reached New York. He made a point of telling Lewis that New Orleans would likely be his final destination and asked the priest about the ferry to the mainland.

On the evening before his departure, Warren walked along the shore. Looking at the stars beginning to sparkle overhead, he comforted himself thinking Dottie might be seeing a similar display in her night sky.

Gazing at the vast expanse of ocean, taking in the sound and smell of the Atlantic, longing to be home, he watched the waves roll and crest before bursting onto the shore.

He listened to the constant music of the sea as birds scampered at the water's edge, leaving soft imprints in the sand. For the first time, Warren felt serene. But when he looked at the water swirling at his feet, his mind turned the brine into blood. He stepped back, swallowing hard, picturing the captain's final moments. Warren turned, heading quickly back to the church.

Once inside the rectory, he summoned the priest.

"I'm afraid I've been too much a burden for you. You have been more than gracious. I will leave you in peace and donate a worthy gift to the church for your kindness."

Lewis said he was happy to attend to him but wanted to know if he could provide spiritual guidance. "You've a troubled soul. It's plain to see. Can I help you find comfort for your spirit, joy in the salvation of our Lord?"

"You've done all you can, more than I could have expected. Please, securing a trunk will be a blessing to me."

After the priest left, Warren paced his room, moving back and forth. He built walls in his mind, brick by brick. Slaves had not been abused, the captain hadn't been killed, and his fellow sailors didn't perish in the storm. He was an independent man, who made his fortune honorably and would serve mankind as a temple of integrity.

He ventured into town to purchase clothes, some necessities, and a small steamer trunk.

The following morning, he boarded a boat taking him to the mainland of North Carolina. He carried his steamer trunk that held nothing but his treasure chest and some blankets to cushion it in place. Warren refused offers to carry the trunk and kept it with him.

When the ship sailed into the inlet reaching the mainland of North Carolina, he waited until the last of the passengers disembarked and then hoisted the steamer trunk, carrying it down the gangplank, ignoring the gaggle of people who pressed themselves on the new arrivals, offering transport and services.

He pushed past them, heading for the offices of the dock, where he asked about transportation to the nearest large city, Greenville. A carriage was arranged, and he travelled the next four hours with his right arm resting firmly on the trunk beside him.

Once there, he made inquiries at the station, learning the better hotels of the town. The nearest was the Albemarle, which sounded suitable to his needs. He checked in and stayed in his room, protecting the treasure until morning.

At nine o'clock, he walked the main street of the city, surveying the four principal banks in its financial district. Warren settled on the Bank of the Carolinas, with large imposing pillars and solid marble stairs. He paced outside for several minutes before going in.

"I'd like to speak to the manager, please."

"About what?" the teller asked.

"I've a deposit to make, fairly substantial."

The clerk's eyebrows went up, and he cocked his head, evaluating Phelps for a moment, then escorted him to an office at the front of the building.

"Mr. Lansing, I've a gentleman inquiring about a deposit."

Lansing was thin, impeccably dressed, with small eyes bracketing a long prominent nose above a dark bushy mustache.

He barely looked up from his desk, raising his eyes only slightly to glance at Warren while he dabbed a pen into an inkwell and entered a note into a ledger before speaking.

"Deposits are entered at the tellers' counter."

"Yes, sir." The clerk waited to escort Warren back to counter.

"It's a significant sum," Warren said.

Lansing placed his pen flat on his desk and sat back on his chair, turning his full attention to Warren.

"And a significant deposit is how much?"

Warren looked at the clerk for several seconds and then back to Lansing, who understood. He waved the clerk away.

"So, what have you brought us?"

"When I say a significant amount, I do mean a considerable value. But I need to know my funds are safe within your walls, and that you can be counted on to handle meaningful transactions."

Lansing sat up higher in his chair, clasping his hands, fingers intertwined, in front of him on his desk.

"You have doubts about the oldest and strongest bank in Greenville? I can assure you we are quite capable of handling any transaction. If you've concerns, there are other banks in town. No one has ever questioned our abilities, Mr. …?"

"Phelps. Warren Phelps."

"Well, Mr. Phelps, there is no more secure institution in all the Carolinas. What exactly are you proposing to deposit?"

"Coins. Gold coins, a large number."

Lansing leaned forward, staring intently into Warren's eyes.

"Coins, you say. What do you consider significant value?"

"More than you might suspect. Provided you can assure me of their safety."

Lansing rose from behind his desk.

"Follow me."

He led Warren behind the teller cages to a staircase descending to a wide basement hallway with a large steel door at the end.

"This, Mr. Phelps, is our safe, the largest, most secure stronghold in the entire state."

He dialed a combination and opened the heavy steel door, revealing a wall of iron bars he made no attempt to open.

"This is where our deposits are safeguarded." He slammed the door shut. "If it's security you want, we're here to serve. What you call a large deposit may be minor to the Bank of the Carolinas."

Warren smiled. "I'm still learning the ways of America, but I think the amount will satisfy your standards. If you would be so kind as to explain how I might make transfers to a bank in another state from time to time, such information will be most helpful, and with that, I'll return this afternoon."

Bible Lessons

In London, Colin was growing more comfortable at St. Anne's, devoting his energies to reading. He mastered the alphabet and was soon reading full basic sentences. Each day he spent a silent hour sitting in the modest library, sounding out words. Writing and penmanship were more of a challenge, but he practiced each letter, over and over, until he could form them clearly.

Deacon Prentiss encouraged Colin's progress in reading and math. More impressive was the boy's ability at music. He struggled to learn the language of musical notation but could sing any string of notes with clarity and precision. He was quickly mastering the piano, playing entirely by ear.

The vibrancy of Colin's voice astonished choirmaster Thompson. He could replicate any pitch, sustaining every sound with velvet modulation. Many of his classmates appreciated his voice, but it caused resentment from some of the boys.

He was called upon to sing solos previously assigned to other students. Colin wasn't sure what all the fuss was about.

To him, music was almost a game: hear the notes, repeat the notes, nothing too difficult.

Religion was a different matter entirely. He chafed under the teachings and Bible readings. The professed piety of his teacher seemed strongly at odds with what he knew of human nature.

Father McCall learned of Colin's resistance and invited him for a walk on a warm spring afternoon. "So, I hear you're struggling with your faith, Colin?"

"I've little experience with God, Father. If he exists, he took my mother, probably my father as well."

"And yet, he brought you here to us."

"I doubt God had anything to do with that." He thought it the height of arrogance for the priest to proclaim himself a personal instrument of God.

"I do read the Bible, Father, what I can of it, in class, listen to the lessons, but I don't feel God's presence, don't see him."

"Tell me, son, do you believe in stars?"

"Of course."

"Good. Look up into the sky and tell me what constellations you see."

Colin glanced perfunctorily into the bright afternoon sky.

"It's daylight. I can't see any stars."

"Ah, so they don't exist?"

"Of course they exist. I just can't see them in daylight."

"Perhaps heaven is like that. You can't see it now, but it exists. You just need the right light to see it."

Colin rolled his eyes, gave the priest a sideways glance, took a deep breath, and gazed at the church tower.

"I've seen stars at night. I know they exist. But I've never seen the slightest sign of God."

"No, but you've seen buds appear on the trees and flowers sprout from the ground. You've seen signs of God's creation all around you: the miracle of birth and the beating of your heart."

"Nature isn't God. It's just nature."

"Then there's no meaning to life, no purpose to our being here?"

Colin thought of the night his mother died, his absent father, the lightermen who tried to harm him, and the arrogance of some boys at school.

"I don't know the meaning of life. But I don't feel any magical force guiding us. There's too much cruelty to convince me someone's directing any of this."

"Be patient, Colin. Open your heart to the idea our Creator has a purpose for your life."

Colin looked at his shoes as they walked in silence.

Father McCall placed his hand on Colin's head and scuffed it across his hair. "I'll teach your Bible class one day soon; perhaps it will help."

Colin tilted his head away and quickened his pace. He didn't think anything the priest could teach would alter his opinion.

During the next few weeks, he nurtured thoughts of leaving St. Anne's. He'd learned to read well enough and decided to visit the wharf where his tin box hung tied beneath the pilings. He might be able to read his father's letter now, though cursive was still a new form for him.

The choir was practicing for a special concert. They were selected to perform at an Easter event to raise money for the Church of England. Bach's Easter Oratorio and his Ascension Oratorio would be sung before some of London's most prominent citizens. Colin was selected to sing a solo that would be the culmination of their performance. He practiced with the choir and separately with the choirmaster until he'd mastered every note.

Five days before the performance, Father McCall came to teach the theology class normally taught by Nicholas Whitehead. Nicholas was a dry teacher who spoke in stiff, judgmental terms, requiring students to repeat whole Bible verses in exact conformance to the text. His teaching technique was a sharp switch to the hands whenever a student hesitated or missed a line. Colin dreaded the lessons.

Father McCall's approach was far different. He strode confidently into the room, then stood stock still, his arms folded across his chest and a broad smile spreading across his face. Students who'd been active and boisterous became silent as they slipped behind their desks and directed attention to the priest.

"Boys, I've a surprise for you today, an exciting prize. It's the most special gift you can imagine, one you'll treasure always.

"We'll divide our class down the middle. Those of you on my left will be the blue team, and those of you on my right will be the green team. Only one team will win. In a second, I'll turn this hourglass over, and you'll each have two minutes to win. One team may not talk to the other, but you can talk amongst your own. Whichever side wins will have the prize; the losing team will have nothing. Is that understood?"

The boys nodded assent.

"Are you ready to play?"

Another roomful of nods.

"Good. Let's begin. We start, now!"

He turned the hourglass upside down and watched as the sand poured from top to bottom.

The classmates looked at each other, bewildered.

"Come, lads, time's running out. Who'll claim the prize?"

"You haven't told us the rules!" A student protested.

"Less than a minute," McCall announced. "Quickly, boys. Time is nearly done."

"You haven't told us what to do!" another shouted.

Colin looked at his teammates and to those across the room. No one seemed to know how to react.

"Hurry, time's almost up."

Some students stood, eager to move at the first instruction; others sat perplexed. The last grains of sand drained from the hourglass. "Times up! Goodness, boys. None of you have claimed the prize. I'm afraid you've all lost."

A chorus of complaints rang out as students protested they'd never been given the rules.

"You didn't tell us what to do!"

"It's not fair. There weren't any instructions!"

The priest smiled. "Oh, you need to know the *rules*!"

He lifted a worn Bible into the air with his right hand. "You didn't know the rules? I'm holding them right here. Do you realize most people live their whole lives not knowing the rules, or not following them? And their lives slip by far too quickly, like the sand in this glass.

Here's the rulebook for life, my boys. This is how your time on earth is measured. The prize is everlasting life, eternal joy. I needn't tell you what the alternative is. Keep by this, and your reward will be assured."

Colin groaned, another trick of religion. But he had to admit the priest had made his point.

The Letter

The next day was Saturday. Colin was on a mission and could barely wait through breakfast before heading to the dock. He understood cursive writing better now, could read most hands, and was eager to finally read his father's letter.

As he approached the docks, Colin became self-conscious of his school uniform. He wasn't invisible the way he'd been when living on the street. Now he felt as if he glowed like a gas lantern in the dirty, smoky streets leading to the water.

The scent of the docks brought a rush of memories and, with them, renewed fears someone may have found his little treasure. At the water's edge, he ducked below the timbers of the wharf, steadying himself against the crossbeam framework. He waved back and forth from one support to the other until he reached the tenth beam. The tin was still attached by its leather straps, though now encrusted with a mixture of rust and green slime.

He carefully untied it, being sure not to let the box fall. He was tempted to open it right then but knew he should wait until back on secure land. When he emerged from underneath, his tin box looked sharply at odds with his nearly clean uniform. He took it to the Thames Street Park, where he could sit on a bench in the early spring air and read the letter at his leisure.

Once there, he uncoiled the rest of the long leather strapping he had once so carefully used to secure it. Then he pried up the lid and stared at his prized belongings. They looked more pathetic than he remembered. A toy soldier, fading into rust, a few marbles, a ribbon from his mother's hair, and the letter. He had placed it in four envelopes to preserve it, but the paper was still damp and fragile. He looked around to be sure he was alone and began to read.

My precious Dottie,

How I long to be with you and Colin. You must wonder at my extended absence. I can only say my time away has been fraught with danger and peril. Much has happened that I am at loss to explain. But fate has conspired to reward me for those struggles in a peculiar way.

It will please you to know I have come into a fortune in America and am determined to put it to the highest use for you and Colin, and for our benevolent Lord.

While I burn to be with you, I have a few months of final business matters to make sure our fortune is secure. I will take the earliest available ship home, where I long to hold you in my arms. You must be patient but a brief bit longer.

When I return, we will begin a new and brighter life. You may rest assured our financial concerns are over. You and Colin need never worry over the struggles of finances again.

Your loving and devoted husband, Warren

Colin read each word slowly. Some of the ink had faded; some was smudged. But he could decipher every word. He remembered the nights his mother would read the letter to herself, how she told him their future would change.

Now he wondered where his father was. If what he wrote was true, why hadn't he returned? Why wasn't he with him? Colin spent nearly an hour sitting on the bench, thinking about his father, inhaling the fragrance of spring flowers, watching the birds, and wondering what to do.

Back at school he sought Father McCall and found him reading in his office. Colin approached the priest and slid the letter across the table to him.

"My father's alive. We have to find him."

McCall looked up, studying Colin before inviting him to sit. He picked the letter up and read it, occasionally glancing at the boy.

"There's a date, over two years ago. If he's not been back since then . . ."

"What if he has been? What if he's here now, looking for me? Please, Father, you have to help me find him!"

"Well, you've a case to make. We will certainly pursue every effort to locate him. But it's been so long."

"We have to start now. Right away!"

"And so we shall, Colin. Allow me to make inquiries. I've a large circle of parishioners and acquaintances. If he's in London, I'll find him for you. But steel yourself, this may take time."

True to his promise, the priest put out the word to the congregation, to his friends, to merchants, city clerks, and to constables he knew. He and Colin began their search back at his old flat. But the previous landlord had departed five months ago. He'd been accused of stealing from residents and barely made it out of town before the authorities came looking to arrest him. The new landlord had never heard of Warren Phelps and had never met Colin.

Father McCall even instructed two teachers to take five of the oldest students on a field trip to Liverpool. They carefully searched passenger manifests to see if the name Warren Phelps appeared but found no such listing. He became convinced Colin's father had never returned. His last thought was to write letters to the Anglican churches in New York, Philadelphia, Boston, and Baltimore. Perhaps they would know the man. He doubted this would bear fruit, but he had made a promise.

Colin developed a new practice of using music to express his emotions. He spent afternoons at the piano playing tunes by ear, mostly his own compositions. With the possibility that his father might be found, Colin developed a light-hearted, optimistic song, almost a welcome march that would celebrate their reunion.

The Search

As weeks went on, Colin grew despondent. He felt nearly as uncomfortable and out of place at St. Anne's as he had in his first week. Knowing his father was alive, that he was out there, gnawed at him. He spent his Saturdays walking the old neighborhood, going into the pubs and coffee shops, searching the streets. He strained his memory to think of any place his father had taken him when they were together.

His father had once taken Colin and his mother to Hyde Park for a picnic on a warm summer evening. Colin remembered kicking a ball with him while his mother sat on a blanket watching, clapping whenever he made a good strike. It was the most secure feeling of his childhood. Colin walked the park trying to find the exact place they'd been.

There had been riots in the park nearly two years ago, just after his mother died. They'd gathered momentum in the successive weeks following the bread riots in East London, the result of a fragile economy after the Crimean War.

That July, thousands of people turned out to protest a proposed sabbath law closing shops and pubs, as well as forbidding transportation services, on Sundays. Crowds came to Hyde Park to jeer at the wealthy and expose their hypocrisy as they clearly enjoyed the good life on the Sabbath. "Go to church!" they yelled at the affluent who rode the park in fancy carriages.

Stones, mud clods, and even clumps of manure were hurled at the conveyances. Pickpockets worked the crowd. Colin saw them at work, learning a thing or two, but never got proficient at the art himself. The protest hadn't ended well; a police brigade charged the mob. Injuries were high on both sides, including forty-nine policemen in need of medical care. Within a day, the bill was withdrawn in Parliament, and tempers subsided.

It was hard for Colin to reconcile the mob anger and the violence with the idyllic time he'd shared there with his parents. He wasn't able to locate the spot where they'd spent that evening. He knew his father wouldn't be there, but he wanted to recapture the feeling.

Days dragged on with no hint of Warren Phelps. Colin lost interest at school, except for morning chapel where he prayed earnestly to see his father again.

If not for the meals, his warm bed, and the headmaster's promise, he'd have left St. Anne's entirely. Colin sat through classes, uninterested, scribbling in his notebook, planning where he might search next. He sought out Father McCall regularly to ask if progress was being made. Had anyone seen him? Did a letter arrive from a church in America? What else could they do now? The priest was always encouraging, though in his heart he thought it a lost cause.

Colin still participated in the choir. He liked the music, and for a time each day, he could concentrate on something other than his father. His skill continued to impress the director and his classmates.

By November, Colin was coming to terms with the fact his father was likely gone forever. He became more engaged with his studies again and with other students. Christmas was on the horizon, with the choir practicing for their major concert of the year. His main challenge would be the particularly difficult solo meant to be the highlight of the holiday performance.

Banker's Night Out

Matthew Commerford adjusted his tie, checking it in the front hall mirror. She'll like this, he thought. A Christmas concert wasn't his first choice for the evening's entertainment, but it's what she wanted, a respectable first date. It wasn't their first time together —he had flirted with her in the lobby of his bank and even walked her three blocks back to her office on one occasion, but this was officially their first evening out. She had mentioned the concert while making her Tuesday deposit, and he immediately recognized it as his opening.

He straightened his tie again, stepping down from the carriage. The gas light outside her door flickered, animating the Christmas wreath. He tapped the brass knocker against the door and stood taller.

It wasn't Margaret who greeted him. Rather it was her brother, Thomas, looking suspicious and protective, who invited him in and showed him to the formal living room.

"Margaret will be down presently. Please, have a chair. I understand, Mr. Commerford, you are in the banking trade."

"The Bank of England, I can comfortably say, is the pinnacle of the 'banking trade,' as you put it."

"Of course, please forgive my informality. The Bank is among our most cherished institutions. Margaret tells me she met you there. Women so rarely conduct financial transactions; however, she rather enjoys delivering deposits for her firm. She tells me you are a vice president in charge of lending practices."

"Yes. A burdensome practice made more tolerable by your sister's visits." Commerford drew an impressive gold watch from his vest pocket, more to show off his elegant possession than to mark the hour. He was about to inquire into what business Thomas was engaged when Margaret descended the stairs. He rose, captivated at her appearance.

During her visits to the bank, she always looked attractive, always drew his attention. Tonight, she appeared radiant. Margaret's eyes sparkled; her hair fell softly around her fresh, smooth, flawless face. Her smile was demure and inviting at the same time.

"My apologies for keeping you waiting. I trust Thomas was able to entertain you?"

"He's been most gracious," taking her hand, and guiding her down the last stair. May I help you with a wrap? It's bracing out there tonight."

A short carriage ride took them to the gleaming new Surrey Music Hall, where they joined a stream of people climbing the stairs. Snow was falling. He extended his arm for her to take and was encouraged when she also reached her other hand up and rested it on his arm. "I've been looking forward to this." She smiled.

The symphony played an opening string of Christmas songs, interspersed with readings from the Scriptures. An intermission was followed by the Boys Choir from Saint Anne's Church. Margaret was enthralled with their performance. Commerford slid sideways glances at her, happy to see her smiling.

Five songs in, a single boy stepped to the front of the choir. He sang a solo, so sweet and pure it captivated the audience. Margaret turned to Matthew with a look of delight. He had to admit this child was something special. When the boy finished, Commerford lifted his printed program, searching for the singer's name.

He noted it and folded the program, but something nagged at him. He opened it again and re-read the name. His fingers drummed his knee. Colin Phelps. Why did that name sound so familiar? Several minutes passed while he tossed the name over and over in his head. He could almost picture a conversation when that name was raised. Who raised it? When did that name come up? Why would anyone have mentioned a child from Saint Anne's?

And then he remembered. *The attorney who opened an account for the benefit of a lost boy. Surely, this couldn't be the same boy, not this child with the angel's voice. He clearly wasn't missing, and yet …*

He reached out, touching Margaret's hand. "Forgive me, please. I shall be back presently. A business matter intrudes. Will you excuse a banker's obligation and wait for me here?" She looked confused but nodded agreement. He hated to leave her side.

Commerford made his way back up the aisle, out to the lobby, and then along the side of the theater to a hallway leading down behind the stage.

He waited in the wing as the choir finished its last two Christmas carols. The audience applauded enthusiastically while choir director Thompson bowed and led the boys offstage. They filed into the wings, and Commerford studied the boy whose solo had enchanted the crowd. From what the banker could recall, the child was about the right age. It seemed difficult to believe this could be him, but then again, lesser chances had paid off.

The banker approached Thompson, introduced himself, and asked if he might have a moment of his time.

"Happy Christmas to you, sir, but I'm a bit consumed now. Boys, hold your lines! We've an encore to perform." He waved his arms, directing the choir back into formation for another stage entrance.

"May we please speak when you're done?" Commerford asked.

"Perhaps tomorrow, at the church, would be more conducive to conversation. I've a band of hooligans who need all my attention this evening."

Commerford handed him a business card.

"Then at your earliest convenience, perhaps? What time shall I call?"

With the time established, Commerford returned to Margaret, as happy with his new discovery as she was with the concert. Perhaps this night was more perfect than anything he could have imagined —in more ways than one.

The next morning, Commerford was waiting outside the barrister's office at King's Hall when attorney George Covington arrived. "I possess information that may lead to the boy you seek. Does the reward still stand?"

"And exactly what boy would that be, Mr. Commerford?"

"You established a trust, funded an account at the bank, for a young Colin Phelps."

"Yes, of course, an odd situation. His father was distraught. I, naturally, complied with his instructions but despaired any hope of finding the lad. You say you know his whereabouts?"

"Do the terms of the reward still stand?"

Covington studied the banker, questioning his character in his mind, then indicated they should take their business into the privacy of his office. Once inside, he motioned for Commerford to sit, and opened a metal file cabinet behind his desk.

"Allow me a moment to review the file." He took his time, ruffling the pages, glancing up above his glasses to evaluate Commerford more closely, before reading the terms.

"A remuneration of five hundred pounds will be paid to the person, or persons, who successfully locates Colin Phelps, formerly of Ashburn Street, son of Warren and Dorothy Phelps, and whose actions result in the direct reunion of father and son." He looked up from the file. "So, yes, the reward still stands. Now, what makes you think you've discovered his whereabouts, and what is his condition?"

"I'm happy to report he's in excellent condition and can be found a short carriage ride from here. I've arranged an appointment within the hour to confirm his presence, and your attendance is most strongly advised."

Confirmation

When they arrived at St. Anne's, Commerford withdrew the concert program from his leather briefcase. He had shown it to the attorney, which heightened his interest but didn't overcome his skepticism. Now he intended to show it to the choir director.

Formalities were barely concluded, and the purpose of their visit barely stated, when the director held up his hand to halt further discussion.

"This is a matter for Father McCall. You gentlemen should remain here until he can join us." With that, he made a quick departure, leaving the banker and attorney to stare at one another, hope growing in their minds.

Father McCall bustled into the room ahead of Deacon Prentiss and the Choir Director. "You're inquiring about Colin Phelps?"

"We are." Commerford and the lawyer stood and shook the priest's hand. "We believe his father is not only alive, but prosperous, and in search of his son."

"And you think he is our Colin Phelps?"

"We believe so and can confirm it with an interview of the lad. Do you happen to know his address before joining your school?"

"In the Broad Street area, originally. His mother had died. Our belief is he lived in the streets and parks for some time before coming under our care."

Prentiss rose to his full height, looking down on his visitors and insisting, "Colin is well provided for here. He has food, shelter, his studies, and his music. He is, in fact, the centerpiece of our choir.

I can see no reason to disrupt his life with us, without first carefully evaluating the consequences."

"The boy has a father. A rather comfortably suited father by all indications. Surely a reunification will be the boy's best course."

"If there *is* a father, why isn't he here himself? What are his circumstances?"

"He returned from sea only to find his wife dead from cholera, and his son missing. Warren spent months searching for the boy but was compelled to end the quest due to pressing business matters. He established a trust for his son and a suitable sum at our bank to provide for his needs. Surely this is in the lad's best interest."

"Colin has been with us nearly five years. Why hasn't his father been here before? Do you even know if he is still alive?"

"We have every reason to believe so."

"That's most curious as I, and indeed most of our church members, have conducted a thorough search for the man. There's been no trace, and no evidence he ever arrived back in London."

"If it is the boy, he can be assured his father searched far and wide for him. He was desolate at having to leave without him. Hence the trust fund he established, and the reward."

"I'll not bring the boy in, and get his hopes up again, until you show without a doubt that you truly know his father is alive, and you know exactly where to find him."

"Of course, Father, we both understand completely, and we're prepared to resolve this to your satisfaction." He withdrew a folder from his briefcase and untied the ribbon that held it shut.

"The man's name is Warren Phelps. His wife, the boy's mother, was Dorothy. Does that ring true to you?"

"You'll find several letters here in his Father's hand, repeatedly asking for word of his son."

Father McCall leaned forward looking at the paperwork in the attorney's hand. He nodded slowly, taking the documents, and bringing them closer to the lamp.

"His father's name is Warren; I'm uncertain as to his mother's name." He read the forms carefully. "I've been to his old home once; it may have been Ashburn Street. I'll ask you gentlemen to stay seated here until I can talk with the boy. Millicent will bring you some tea."

He got up to leave, with Prentiss trailing right behind. Once in the hallway, Prentiss touched the priest's elbow.

"Colin's safe here, getting his education. *We're* his home now. We know nothing about his father and have no reason to believe he'll properly care for the lad. Perhaps we should wait, take our time."

"I know how much he means to you and the choir, but I've made a promise to the boy, and I'm committed to see him united with his father. Perhaps you should keep the gentlemen company while they wait."

Colin sat in class conjugating Latin verbs. McCall opened the door, held his arm out to the boy, gesturing with his index finger for him to follow into the hall.

They walked silently to the Headmaster's office. Colin turned to the priest several times as they walked, hoping for an explanation. McCall held his hands clasped behind his back and tilted his head toward the ceiling as if contemplating something serious. It made Colin apprehensive. Once in the office, McCall asked the boy to sit.

"As you know, we're making every attempt to find your father. I seem to have forgotten your mother's name, I'm sorry to say."

"Dottie. Dorothy actually," Colin said, wondering where this was going.

"We visited your old home, but I can't recall the name of your street."

"Ashburn."

"Of course. I should have remembered." He nodded his head, looked directly at Colin with an encouraging smile. "I may have some news for you."

A New Life Awaits

IN the blink of an eye, Colin went from a poor street urchin, supported by the church, to a relatively affluent young man — more importantly, a young man with a father, whose whereabouts he finally knew.

Attorney George Covington explained that Warren Phelps wrote every few weeks, inquiring into the progress of finding his son. For the last two years, those letters had come from the same address in Boston, Massachusetts. He also explained Warren had, indeed, been in London searching for his son. He hadn't been on any ship's passenger manifest because he'd signed on as crew to speed his voyage home on the first available ship.

It was agreed two letters would be immediately dispatched to Boston. The first, from the attorney's hand announcing Colin had been found. The second, from Colin himself:

My dear father,

You can't imagine how my heart leapt at discovering you have been alive and searching for me. Please know I am well and have been searching for you too. It has been my good fortune to be taken in by Father McCall and St. Anne's Church, where my education has advanced. It is through their grace, and patience, I can write to you in my own hand. We are all eager to know if I should embark immediately for Boston, or if you will return for me in London. Our reunion shall be the answer to all my prayers.

Your loving son, Colin

For the time being, Colin would remain at St. Anne's until word was received. His bank balance now allowed him to purchase clothes and other items he would need to start his new life. His first purchase was a book about the United States, complete with maps of the country. At the suggestion of Deacon Prentiss, he bought works by two American authors, Nathanial Hawthorne, and Henry David Thoreau, both of whom lived in Massachusetts.

Colin became more energized and fully engaged in his studies. He was determined to make his father proud, to absorb as much knowledge as possible. He read voraciously and engaged in long conversations with the priests and teachers about life, philosophy, science, and religion.

He remarked to Father McCall that science seemed in contradiction to religion. Biology, after all, held no proof of life hereafter.

"Is that so?" McCall asked. He went to the board and drew three objects: an acorn, a tadpole, and a caterpillar. "What are these items?"

Colin named each with growing skepticism of the cleric's intent.

"And, what does a tiny acorn become?"

The boy looked at the ceiling and sighed.

"A tree, Father."

"Not just any tree, Colin, a mighty oak tree, of enormous height. And what will become of our tadpole here?"

"It will become a frog," losing patience.

"Good, and this fuzzy caterpillar?"

"A butterfly."

"Precisely. Each of these tiny beings can change miraculously into something far greater than its size or understanding. Do you think a tadpole has any idea it will develop legs and leap great distances, or that a caterpillar ever dreams it will fly some day? Such transformations! I like to think our bodies are like a cocoon from which, if we are careful with our lives, we will emerge as heavenly beings."

"It's a nice theory, Father. I hope you're right." He'd learned to just accept the priest's lessons and not to argue his points.

Colin's work with the choir progressed. The choirmaster bemoaned the impending loss of his star vocalist. He began rehearsing other boys, but none came close to Colin in ability or tone.

Three weeks after the letters were dispatched, Father McCall accompanied Colin to Mr. Commerford's office in the bank. They sought assurances their letters were delivered. Colin said he should have been permitted to deliver the letters himself, to personally hand them to his father. They wondered now if waiting for a reply only delayed matters if, in fact, the boy's father wanted him to come directly to Boston.

Another fear crept into Colin's heart. What if his father had died? The banker could only advise patience. "Give it time, lad. Your father will respond the moment he learns you are found."

Days dragged on. Waiting for word from America, Colin's spirits faltered. What if his father was content with his new life in a new country, perhaps with a new family? What if his father insisted he remain in London under the care of St. Anne's? He forced himself to push the ideas aside, instead picturing the outstretched arms of his father. Colin suddenly realized how hard it was to picture his father's face. He was so young the last time they were together.

Valentine's Day, 1858

SUNDAY, February 14, 1858, was Valentine's Day. Parishioners filled the church to capacity. Each woman was given a red carnation as she entered. Father McCall's sermon naturally focused on love. He spoke for thirty minutes before making his summation:

"How important is love? Our Savior has provided a simple answer. The last example and the last commandment to his disciples was inordinately clear, and his only message was love.

"Recall the Last Supper, our Savior kneeling before his apostles, washing their feet, something only the lowest servant would do. And when he was done, he asked them, Do you realize what I've done for you?

"As I have served you, so should you serve one another. Moments later, he gave his last commandment: Love one another. As I have loved you, so shall you love one another. My dear friends, that is the heart of Christianity. Keep Him in your hearts, keep each other in your hearts, this Valentine's Day, and everyday hereafter."

As the service ended, parishioners began filing slowly out of the church. The choir stood to sing an exit hymn, Charles Wesley's "Love Divine, All Loves Excelling."

A gentleman entered the back of the church, holding a leather-bound journal under his arm. He scanned the faces of the boys twice before resting his eyes on Colin. A smile spread across his face as he walked down the aisle, threading his way through the exiting congregants, picking up his pace.

Colin was in mid-verse when he saw the man approach. He mouthed words without singing them. Could this be?

Warren Phelps stopped in front of the choir, directly facing Colin. He nodded his head and held his arms out wide. The boy couldn't move at first, then left his place and stepped down from the rostrum. He gave a hesitant smile and rushed into his father's arms.

Warren embraced his son, lifted him off the marble floor, and kissed his cheek. "My son, my precious son!"

He reached into his pocket, brought out a frayed, soft, blue woolen mitten, and held it out to his son. "You've always been with me, always in my heart."

Colin looked at the mitten, remembering it from long ago, then looked in his father's eyes and said, "I knew you'd come."

A Long Goodbye

Rules Restaurant on Maiden Lane, Covent Garden, was nearly a hundred years old, with a steady clientele of London's most fashionable crowd. Members of the Royal Family, lawyers, politicians, and journalists mingled with actors and authors.

Charles Dickens often enjoyed the meat pies and oysters of the establishment. The author sat two tables away, savoring his meal and reveling in an animated conversation. Dickens caught the attention of Father McCall, but Warren and Colin were oblivious to his presence.

They had plans to discuss. Colin peppered his father with constant questions about life in America. His father was more occupied with thanking the priest for sheltering and caring for his boy.

"It has always been my intention to reward anyone who found Colin. While our banker friend has rightfully claimed that, I have a larger reward I wish to bestow upon your church. In addition to the 1,500 pounds you received this afternoon, I've established a fund through the Bank of England to pay a steady yearly sum to St. Anne's. While you remain at her helm, you may request and direct the funds as you see fit. When you depart the church, in any fashion, the trust will pay an annual amount each January to help support your school."

The priest was overwhelmed. "You should know Colin has been far more a blessing than a burden for St. Anne's. He's always been headstrong, but he's applied himself well, and contributed mightily to our choir. His leaving is a great loss. He will be missed."

Colin felt anxious, unworthy of praise, and eager to be alone with his father, to learn more about the country that would be his new home. He fingered the soft linen tablecloth with his right hand and stared at the diners across the room, well-dressed, seemingly content with their lives, drinking wine from crystal glasses, cutting into prime rib with fine silverware.

He remembered being out on the streets, in the cold, peering through windows, watching satisfied patrons enjoying their meals. How distant that seemed now. Could this really be his new lot in life?

His thoughts were interrupted when a white-gloved waiter appeared with a large plate of cherry cobbler. He placed it in front of Colin. The boy looked up at his father, who smiled and said, "You are one of life's greatest victories, son. You should have dessert every night." Colin beamed and picked up his fork.

Plans were finalized. Warren Phelps was, after all, a businessman now, with responsibilities in Boston. He and Colin would begin the trip to America before the week was out.

He had explained his business ventures to his son. He controlled two enterprises in Boston, the first being a machine shop fabricating parts for America's growing railroad business and components for ships and boilers. His second business, the one occupying most of his heart, was a printing press. The business took on a variety of jobs, but the one he was passionate about was a weekly newspaper, *The Liberator*, written by a staunch abolitionist, William Lloyd Garrison.

After dinner, their carriage delivered them to the Richmond Hotel. The driver grabbed Colin's new leather suitcase, the one holding the sum total of all his possessions, and put it in the hands of a valet who stood at attention, while another held the door open for the boy and his father.

Colin looked down at his new shoes as he walked on the polished white marble floor, then up at the gas chandeliers with their warm, welcoming light. People were elegantly attired. A group of men stood smoking cigars, laughing as they turned their attention to a slender young woman crossing the lobby holding a small white dog. The valet led the way to a black marble staircase with a shining brass banister.

In their room, Colin ran his hand across the bedspread of the tall four poster, the largest bed he'd ever seen. Two candy mints were on his pillow and the pillow of his father's matching bed.

He and his father talked for hours. Colin learned things he'd never known about his family. He had an unquenchable need to discover everything about his father's life: how he and his mother met, what it was like at sea, what America was like.

Warren spoke openly, sharing details, including memories of the night Colin was born and their early times together. He was purposely vague about his days in America.

"You have her eyes, you know. I should never have left. I never thought I'd lose her and nearly lose you. Can you forgive me?"

"If you'd stayed, you would likely have died from cholera as well. Fate took you away so you could be spared, so you could come back and find me."

There was a long pause, and then his father said, "You've inherited more than her eyes. There was a wisdom about her that now lives in you." He paused. "We'll be leaving London, perhaps forever. What would you like to see before we depart?" He helped his son list the places he'd most want to see before leaving London.

Colin barely slept. Anxiety swept over him. He thought of Father McCall, his classmates, his teachers. Over the past years, they had become his home. The school where he'd learned so much, experienced so much, would be lost to him. Being with his father meant giving up everything and everyone he knew. It meant replacing all he was comfortable with in England. What if he hated America? What if Americans hated him? Perhaps he should stay in London. He got out from under the covers, knelt beside the bed, and prayed God would bless him and keep him safe.

The next day was spent shopping, and their last four days were devoted to visiting London's special places: Buckingham Palace, Trafalgar Square, the St. Stephens Tower (later nicknamed Big Ben), which was nearly complete. The largest clock in the world, with its nine-foot hour hand and fourteen-foot minute hand, was a marvel. The Latin inscription under the dial read, "O Lord, keep safe our Queen Victoria the First." Parliament was in session, and they watched speeches from the gallery of the House of Commons. The Crystal Palace built in Hyde Park for the Great Exhibition of 1851 had been moved to South London but was high on the list of places to see. The Tower of London was next, with its crown jewels, and finally a day of museums.

"You should know this city, your country. It's part of who you are, and you may want to come back someday. If not, at least you'll know where you're from."

Their final stop was Dottie's grave in Norwood. Warren knew the way by heart and held Colin's hand as he guided him to the site. The boy clutched a bouquet of flowers in his other hand.

Her previous, temporary, marker had been replaced by a handsome marble headstone with intricate scrolling surrounding a graceful carved rose. The inscription below her name read: "Precious wife, loving mother. Lost too soon, but never forgotten."

The boy carefully placed the flowers in front of the stone; then father and son knelt to pray. Warren put his hand on top of the marker. Colin placed his on top of his father's.

After several minutes of silence, Warren looked at his son and said, "We will never forget her. She'll be watching us, wanting the best for us, guiding us to live righteous lives."

Colin nodded and wiped a tear from his eye, saying a silent goodbye, with a solemn promise to be good.

Ocean Voyage

They booked passage to New York on *The Southampton.* The first two days at sea were exhilarating for Colin, the fulfillment of a long-held dream. He loved walking the deck, feeling the ocean breeze and the sunlight, leaning on the rail watching for sea life and ships.

On the third day, the weather changed. Winds whipped up, creating large dark waves that crashed against the ship as it rocked and fell.

The walls of his cabin seemed to spin, his head lost its guideposts, and his legs buckled as he staggered to his bunk. His stomach sought to rise into his mouth. It was all he could do to keep its contents down. He lay down, his hands clasped over his chest, sweat dripping from his forehead. When he could bear it no longer, he rolled over, leaned away from the bed, and spewed his breakfast onto the cabin floor.

His father cleaned up the mess, then sat on the edge of the bed, holding a damp washcloth over the boy's eyes with one hand and a glass of water in the other.

"You've got to drink something, or you'll be dehydrated. Can you sit up?"

Colin groaned, put one hand on the bed, and pushed up with it, turning sideways, rising almost to a sitting position. His body swayed forward, and then he fell back onto the bunk.

Warren tried not to laugh, remembering the same feeling from his first voyage.

"This will pass, son. Just hold on a bit longer." He brought the glass to his son's lips and coaxed a few sips into him before the boy turned his head away. Colin rolled on to his stomach, his arms stretched out, clenching the mattress tightly on both sides, as if to keep from falling off.

By morning, the sea had calmed. Colin's stability was returning. A steward brought beef broth and toast, which agreed with him well. By midday, he could step out on deck again.

He wasn't secure enough to lean on the rail and watch the bubbling white foam trailing away from the ship's side, so he nestled onto a deckchair, wrapped a blanket around himself, and opened his book on America. He studied the maps, imagining what this new landscape would look like in person.

His father found him there. "After last night, I'm glad we didn't buy you Moby Dick. Now, there's a story of adventures at sea! How're you doing?"

"Better now, Father. May I ask you something?"

"Of course."

"Why did you take so long to return? Is there something about America that tied you there? I'm not meaning any judgment, just trying to understand, if you're willing to say."

Warren sat on the edge of the adjoining deckchair and clasped his hands in front of him. "You've every reason to ask. I've been wanting to tell you, to explain, but the circumstances have not been easy."

He paused, staring into the sky for several seconds before looking back at his son.

"I signed on for a two-year contract as a merchant seaman on a cargo ship. The captain's intent was to sell cargo in New York, take on goods for England, and complete that business four times in two years. The very first year's voyage ended badly.

"Our goods sold poorly in New York. To improve our fortunes, the captain ordered us to set sail to Savannah where cotton could be had more cheaply, and our manifest might draw a higher price.

"The southern states are not like the north. Negroes are still held as slaves, still treated like animals, or worse. I saw shocking things, experiences, and faces I shall never forget. When the captain sought to use those poor souls as free labor against his crew, I demanded my wages and parted company.

"With little to my name, and no immediate way home, I worked my way north, saving my earnings, looking for ways to advance, not for me, but for you and your mum.

"I was foolish enough to think I should secure our finances before coming home for you. My promise to your mother was that I would make a better life for both of you.

"I learned land-based trades so I wouldn't ever have to leave you and Dottie for the sea again. In Connecticut, I worked at the Colt Armory and learned machinery skills. Learned them so well, I was able to buy into a Boston metal and machine shop. As soon as it was up and sufficiently on its feet, I boarded the next available ship to England.

"Returned only to find my precious wife buried, and you lost to who knows where. I spent months searching for you.

"Old Mr. Blessing was made to suffer for throwing you out, and I pressed him into the search for you as well. It broke my heart to leave again. I despaired of ever finding you. Every month, I wrote to the attorney, seeking any possible clues of finding you. When your letter arrived, I put my affairs in order and signed on to the first ship that would bring me home."

Colin, again, suspected there was more his father wasn't saying, but he sat up and placed a hand on his father's arm. "You didn't give up. You found me, and had you stayed, the sickness that took mother would have surely taken you as well. Can you tell me more of what our home in Boston is like?"

"First, let me tell you about New York. We'll be there soon."

New York

New York wasn't like London. Its docks teamed with workers speaking so many languages, it sounded like the Tower of Babel. Polish, Italian, Gaelic, and German languages clashed with one another. The activity was furious. Workers hurried to compete against other crews, far different from the relaxed, organized approach of dock workers in Liverpool or the lightermen on the Thames in London.

America looked as if all of Europe had been mashed together on its concrete and wooden wharfs. Cargo moved from one set of strong arms to the next as crews worked with impressive speed, shuttling crates and bags from the ship to a constant line of horse-drawn wagons. Men winched ropes, pulling cables, lifting large containers up from the ship's deck, swinging them over the dock and landing them gently onto its surface. Seagulls swept overhead; cats swerved their way to the scent of fish. The activity that had seemed so chaotic at its start now functioned like a well-choreographed dance.

Colin took in the whole scene as he, and his father disembarked. Near the bottom of the gangplank, a small band played music for arriving passengers, and barkers hawked tours and hotels. Two men in bowler hats and vests passed out flyers, shouting promises that Tammany Hall could get them jobs and citizenship.

"Are ya Irish?" they called as Warren and Colin passed.

Clearing customs took over two hours, but they finally strode into the sunshine of a New York afternoon. As they waited for a cab, Colin put his new leather bag on a stair step. He felt the ground shifting under him. The sea legs he'd developed onboard hadn't adjusted to dry land. He bent to tie his shoe. Within seconds, a young boy bounded behind him, scooped up the bag, and ran full speed down the street.

Colin shouted as he, and his father tore after the boy. When they passed an alley, a man rushed out, grabbed Warren's suitcase from his hand, then ran the opposite direction, darted across the cobblestone in front of a horse-drawn cab, and disappeared down a side street. Warren started after him, but his son was already far down the street in pursuit of his own bag. Warren turned and chased after the felon who had stolen Colin's.

Colin was gaining on the boy, who ran with an awkward gait, almost as if one leg was a bit shorter than the other. When he was close upon him, the robber stopped abruptly, turned, and swung the suitcase hard across Colin's face. Colin staggered backwards, blood flowing from his nose, which he wiped with his shirt sleeve while regaining his balance. He took up pursuit again, and again the assailant turned to swing the bag. This time, Colin caught it and pulled hard on his end while his foe pulled equally hard from his.

They spun counterclockwise until Colin gave a final strong yank, sending the boy off-balance and down to the ground. Colin stood, breathing hard, while his father ran up and immediately pinned the felon to the street.

The boy lay squealing, demanding to be let up. Warren raised his fist, but Colin grabbed his arm, stopping him. He was staring at urchin's shoes. One was missing a heel. The other had been completely worn away at the front, so his toes stuck out.

"Just hold him for a minute."

Colin bent down, opening his suitcase. He felt through his belongings and took out two pair of socks and a brand-new pair of shoes, probably one size too large for the boy.

"Here, take these. Did you ever think people might offer help if you'd ask instead of stealing from them?"

Warren looked up at his son in surprise.

"Don't do that, son. He's a thief! He may have broken your nose."

"He needs them more than I do. Let him up."

His father slowly stood, keeping one hand on the boy's collar, lifting him as he rose, still staring at Colin to see if his son was serious. Colin placed the shoes and socks in his assailant's hand, then picked up his bag, and turned back toward their starting point. His father gave a slight shrug, released his grip, pushed the offender away, and followed his son.

Back at the taxi stand, Warren stared down the side street where his own bag had disappeared, knowing it was gone for good. Well, he thought, it's only clothes. They explained what had happened to the cab driver and asked where they could locate a police officer.

"Welcome to New York," was all he said, along with an assurance the police would do nothing to search for his belongings.

Their plan had been to spend a few days in the city, taking in its newly opened Central Park, staying at a nice hotel, and enjoying some of New York's finer restaurants. Now, they had little interest in anything other than boarding a train for Boston.

They spent one night at the Metropolitan Hotel on the corner of Broadway and Prince Streets. It was built in an elegant Romanesque style with fine furnishings imported from Europe, including the largest plate-glass mirrors in the United States. The furnishings alone were estimated to have cost over $200,000 when the hotel was built in 1852.

The Metropolitan operated on the American Plan, offering three full meals a day. However, without his suitcase, Warren didn't have clothes sufficient for the hotel's elegant restaurant. Colin's nose was swollen, and the skin under his eyes was turning dark, hardly the look expected in a fine dining room. Instead, they walked to a more modest eatery several blocks away, where Colin studied the diners with great interest to see how real Americans looked and acted.

Warren assured his son America was not teeming with thieves and criminals. Boston, he said, would provide a safe, secure home.

"You shouldn't have given him your shoes. He's a robber. It won't deter him in the future. It's more likely to encourage his thievery. Why would you do that?"

"I used to be that boy. Not that I ever robbed anyone, well, not like that. He's young enough; he still might straighten out. Perhaps someone will take him in."

His father felt a pang of guilt. "You were out on the street because I was over here. It's my fault you suffered."

"We're together now. That's all I care about."

They sat quietly waiting for their food.

"I hope you're right about that boy. I hope someone does take him in, turns his life around."

Colin sipped his tea, held the cup in his hands, looking over it into his father's eyes, and said, "I wonder about Mom; do you think she's forgotten us?"

"No, I think she's happy, and she watches over us to make sure we're safe. We're still holding her in our hearts while we live. I'm sure she's smiling at us now."

"Father McCall told me something I can't forget."

"Yes, what's that?"

"He said when a person goes to heaven, after his body's gone, and with no earthly cares to distract him, he remembers every single second of his life. The good and the bad. For all eternity.

"He said we'd remember every time we cared for someone, every time we helped them, and sacrificed for them. And we'd have those memories always, forever. We'd even know exactly how we made other people feel. That's part of our heaven.

"But he also said we'd remember every bad thing we'd ever done. Every time we could have helped but didn't, each time we hurt someone's feelings, stole from them, or ruined their plans. And we'll know exactly how we made each of them feel, forever. It's like constructing your heaven and hell right here during your life. McCall said all we can accumulate on earth are memories, and it's up to us to gather as many good, kind ones as we can. Do you think it's true?"

Warren shivered; a quick vision of the slave trade, and the image of Captain Winters sinking below the waves, flashed across his mind. He brushed his hand over his eyes and quickly drew it down his face, resting his fingers on his neck.

"I think when we're gone, we'll have no use for this earth, and won't give it a thought as we unite with your mother, enjoying the pleasures of heaven."

Their food arrived. Colin was starving and tore into his roast beef, butter beans, and potatoes. His father sat watching him, then stared into the candle's flame, hoping the priest was wrong.

Boston

THE next morning, Warren shopped to replace essentials while Colin slept in at the hotel. When he woke, he finished packing and stood by the window watching America flow by below. The energy of New Yorkers definitely surpassed what he was accustomed to in London. It was as if each one had an urgent personal mission to accomplish.

Colin took his suitcase and headed to the lobby, still enjoying the brilliant experience of an elevator ride. He acknowledged the operator and asked if Central Park was close by.

"Tis as close as it's ever been. Hasn't moved a bit." An Irish brogue.

Colin laughed. "Is it in walking distance?"

"I don't know a place dat isn't, if you've the legs for it."

"Where are you from?"

"Galway. God's garden by the sea."

"Have you been here long?"

The operator shrugged. "Long enough to get used to it. Long enough our whole family was evicted to make way for the new park. Our home was Seneca Village, Irish, Blacks and a smattering of Germans. A poor lot, but it was ours, and they just took it away."

When the elevator reached the lobby, Colin could barely get out before three men hustled in, as if steak and lobsters were being served for free in the little cage. He suspected they shared his delight in this new mobile contraption.

Colin sat in the lobby on a scarlet velvet sofa, watching the activity around him. He listened to the way people spoke and watched how they interacted, how they dressed, and how they moved.

His father arrived, having purchased tickets for the three o'clock train to Boston, allowing them just enough time for a ride through Central Park.

Irish immigrants and free Blacks had lived on the land for over fifty years, raising livestock and building churches, schools, and even cemeteries. The city claimed the land by eminent domain and swept its residents away.

Only a portion of the 843 acres had been opened, but New York was proud of its fresh green jewel, so it was deemed worth seeing. Colin thought it a poor comparison to the parks and gardens of London. His father explained Boston Common was the first city park in America, predating New York's by over two hundred years.

Their train ride to Boston provided another opportunity to soak in American culture. Colin was struck by the informality of the passengers. They seemed more direct, and certainly more opinionated, than those he was accustomed to at home. He found it refreshing.

He'd fallen asleep during the last hour of their journey. His father woke him with the words, "We're home." It was an assurance he'd waited for most of his life.

A man met them at the station. Joseph Newton worked at the Phelps foundry and served as Warren's personal secretary and business manager. He was young, tall, and lanky, with an attitude vacillating between attentive servitude and business efficiency. He appeared to have a flair for the latest fashion and took pride in his personal appearance. His thick, red-brown hair and mustache reminded Colin of a squirrel.

Newton was a constant frenzy of activity, rushing across the railway platform to greet them, stretching out his right arm to shake Warren's hand while simultaneously taking his employer's suitcase with his left.

"And this must be him," he smiled turning to Colin. "We've waited a long time for this, boy. You've answered your father's most fervent prayer. Permit me to introduce myself, Joseph Newton, secretary to your father and treasurer to Phelps Industries."

He shook Colin's hand with a cold grip, then efficiently took possession of his suitcase. He was about to turn, but stopped, dropped both cases, and bent with his hands on his knees, looking intently into Colin's face and then into Warren's.

"He's black and blue! Has there been trouble?"

"A scuffle in New York. Colin gave better than he got, and a thief was taught a lesson."

"We'll not have any such thing here in Boston. You can rely on me for protection, lad."

Colin doubted this frenzied squirrel could offer much protection, but he smiled and said, "Much obliged. Good to meet you." He hadn't heard the term "Phelps Industries" before; it sounded important. He smiled.

"Well, Colin, are you ready to see our home?"

A Room of His Own

Home was a modest brick and stone townhouse on Washington Street, hardly the mansion of an "industrialist." But it was a significant improvement from the flat he'd been thrown out of in London.

Newton followed them up the steps and into the foyer with their luggage. Once inside, he directed Warren's attention to a stack of envelopes on the front hall table. "The mail's been piling up. It's good you're home; some of these demand immediate attention."

"Nothing deserves my attention more than my son. Leave us some time together. I promise to return to business early in the morning."

Newton started to say there were matters to address, but Warren cut him off.

"Tomorrow morning is soon enough. I'll be ready for you at six o'clock."

"Very well," he sighed. "Six o'clock."

He nodded to Colin, turned swiftly, and dashed through the door.

"Newton means well, but he's all business. Some days I feel I work for him and not the other way around. Come. I'll show you your room."

His bedroom was the first door at the top of the stairs. Colin thought of his old cot at St. Anne's, also at the top of the stairs, but this was all his, a room of his own. The bed was large and firm with several pillows and a thick blue and white comforter; a dresser with a tall mirror stood against one wall, an armoire for his clothes on the other, next to a window, framed by curtains matching his bedspread. The whole room, its furniture and rug, smelled new.

A map of London hung near the door. Colin unpacked, placing the last item, his small, old, blue mitten, on one of the curved wooden ornaments spreading from either side of the mirror. He took the leather strap off of his neck, thinking to place it and his mother's ring on the other peg, hesitated, then put it back around his neck.

Dinner was at Durgin-Park in the Faneuil Hall Marketplace, where his father's promise of "the most delicious chowder and the most generous portion of prime rib" proved accurate. Warren chose it as an appropriate place to explain what he knew of Boston's history, but mostly as a suitable backdrop to explain his strong views on slavery. John Durgin greeted Warren as if he was an old friend.

"Perhaps you'll tell my son how your country's rebellion against ours started here, you and all your rebellious grandfathers."

Durgin laughed and said he couldn't take much credit for it himself, but Samuel Adams and his compatriots had fully inspired the revolution with speeches just outside these doors at Faneuil Hall. "You Brits put up a good fight but were no match for us colonists."

"No need to rub old wounds," Warren laughed. "I'm about to acquaint my son with America's limitations on freedom and liberty."

"So, you've not softened your stance on slavery, I see."

"Nor shall I. When I think …"

Durgin held up his hand to stop him. "I've heard your speech before. Perhaps you should concentrate on things you can personally influence. This argument never ends." He rested a hand on Colin's shoulder. "I pray you can temper your father's passion. It would do him good." He smiled at them both and headed off to greet another group of diners.

"You hear him? Even in New England, men are so accustomed to slavery they're no longer moved by it. And here, where they demanded equality for all, they never meant the black man. They may as well have written 'Let the slave remain a slave' in their Constitution."

Colin shifted uncomfortably in his chair. He knew his father abhorred slavery but hadn't realized how virulent his opinions had become. It seemed strange that his father, having come from England, and never having lived in a slave state, should take the issue so firmly to heart. He wanted to enjoy his father's company without controversy or anguish.

Warren sensed his son's concern and said, "There's more I want to acquaint you with, but not tonight. Do you know about baseball?"

"Like rounders, but American style?"

"Somewhat. It's all the rage in New York now. In Brooklyn, they're even charging admission to watch a game. Boston is fielding several teams."

They were fatigued after a long day of activities, and a satisfying meal. Both wanted to turn in early. Colin looked forward to spending the first night in his new room.

Phelps Industries

THE next morning, Warren woke his son at five o'clock. "Time to see our family business, Colin."

After a quick breakfast of scrambled eggs and toast with jam, they headed out, turning onto Essex Street, then walking several blocks to the edge of the rail lines. Even at that early hour, the street was busy, with large wagons making deliveries, people hurrying to work, men smoking cigars and reading their newspapers as they walked, carefully stepping over scattered mounds of horse manure. One boy led two goats tethered together, with sacks on their backs bulging with fruit he sold from shop to shop.

A large warehouse abutted the tracks. The narrow building crackled with activity. Hammers shaped metal, blast furnaces sparked and roared, machines scraped iron, crates groaned and banged as they were unloaded from delivery wagons, and workers shouted above the noise. The building smelled of ash, metal, and oil.

Warren proudly showed Colin the various stations where parts were fashioned for railroad cars, where casings were crafted for steamships, and where sundry parts were filed and polished for final delivery. Colin was impressed with the level of activity. Could all these people work for his father? Phelps Industries was suddenly real.

Newton hurried to greet them as soon as their tour ended. He pulled Warren aside and spoke slowly for a change.

"Sir, it may not be safe having your son here; there's so much that could harm him in the metal shop. Surely, he'd benefit from being in school. Shall I arrange his enrollment for you? I'm certain Boston Latin is the right school for a boy his age. Really the only proper choice, and it's close by, on Bedford Street."

"There's time enough for that. For now, I'm determined to show him every aspect of my life and business affairs. It's important that Colin see the responsibilities for which his education will prepare him."

Newton gave an uncomfortable look, as if being asked to let a wet dog onto a new silk sofa, but smiled at the boy and said, "Of course. All in due time."

THE LIBERATOR

JUST before noon, Warren told his son, "It's time you see our printing business, the place where we're shaping the minds of America."

A carriage ride through the crowded streets took them to 21 Cornhill Street, a three-story brick building with a large bay window and a bright red door where a sign overhead said: J.B. Jerrington & Son, Printers. Warren pointed to it and said, "The banks tried to foreclose, but I've loaned them funds to continue."

When they entered, a burly man with a wild beard stood, placing his hand over a pistol on the table in front of him. He relaxed and smiled when he recognized Warren Phelps.

Inside room number 6, Colin saw a cluttered office with piles of old newspapers and printing supplies crammed into every available space. The sound of machinery chugged from the back room. The odor of ink and paper saturated the air. Warren lifted a newspaper from the top of the pile and handed it to Colin.

"*The Liberator*," he explained. "Written by William Lloyd Garrison himself! The single strongest voice of reason and compassion that rings throughout this nation."

Colin's look implied he wasn't sure he should be impressed. He studied the paper's logo: an illustration of a slave auction on the upper left, a medallion in the center depicting Christ blessing a slave while his master cowers in shame, and to the right, an illustration of slaves welcoming freedom. The words below proclaimed, "Our Country is the World, Our Countrymen are all Mankind." A ribbon snaked throughout the picture, displaying the words "Thou Shall Love Thy Neighbor as Thyself."

A column on the left noted the paper was published every Friday under the subscription terms of $2.50 per annum.

"We help fund the publication for Mr. Garrison and his general agent, Mr. Wallcut. Come, I want you to meet Ben."

They went around the counter to the loud back room and had barely set foot across the threshold when a large, muscular African American wearing blue coveralls over a stained white undershirt stepped in front of the printing press to greet them.

"Come to visit your investment, Mr. Phelps?" he asked, wiping ink from his hands with a rag.

"Come to introduce you to my son, Ben." Warren smiled proudly. "Colin, this is Benedictus Smith. Ben, allow me to present Colin Phelps to your acquaintance."

Ben put his balled fists onto his hips and whistled.

"Lord be praised! I heard you gone all t' way to London, and now here ya be, with dis fine look'n' young man." He stretched out his muscular arm and shook Colin's hand, like a leopard capturing a mouse. The boy's white hand felt small and weak under the firm pressure of Ben's strong grasp. Colin realized he'd never touched a Negro before. He had seen some in London, and during their trip, but couldn't recall ever having even spoken with one.

"What news have you found for this edition? May we see?"

"More o' the same, only worse I 'spect." He took a paper from the top of a freshly printed stack and pointed to an article in the upper left-hand side. "See what our fine enlightened brothers are plott'n' in California for us."

Warren took the newspaper and moved closer to the gas lamp to read the article. He glanced up several times as if questioning what he read could be true.

The following is a literal copy of a bill drawn up and about to be introduced in the California Assembly by an honest miner—a member of the Lower House:

AN ACT:

To prevent niggers from coming to Kallyforny.

The people of the State of Kallyforny represented in Senit and Assembly, do enact as follows:

Section 1. No nigger not now an inhabitant uv, in, and legal voter of this stait, shall be permitted to liv, reside or stay in this stait any longer.

Section 2. Enny nigger hoo wilfully or axidently violates the first seckshun of this act shall be transported from this stait and sold to the highest bidder, Chinamen excluded.

Section 3. Niggers who cum with their masters to sojourn temporarily shall not be included in the provisions uv this act; provided such sojourning doesn't exceed 40 years.

Section 4. All ackts or parts of ackts contraventin this, is repeeled.

Enacting Claws: A nigger is herbi deklared an obnokshus newsans, not to be permitted, and every sheriff in this stait may be a nigger driver if he chuses.

(The Liberator, vol. XVIII, no. 30 July 23, 1858)

"I see Mr. Garrison has not added a comment as none is necessary," Warren said soberly.

"And that from our 31st State, not yet eight years old, Mr. Phelps."

"Well, it won't pass. It cannot pass."

"I 'spect you may hold your white brethren in higher esteem than they are worth."

"Perhaps *The Liberator* could be sent to California?"

"If you've the money for it. You know full out our circulation stands at 3,000 copies, most read by Negroes here in New England. Sends it to da White House and state capitals, but who knows if they reads it. Californians might just wipe their lily-white asses with it. Don't mean no disrespect; your support outshines most folks I know."

"I hope my fervor does as well. There may be no hope for any of us, Ben, if California's assembly ever takes this up. To think such an act, drafted by an imbecile, could even be introduced in a free state."

"Take heart in Minnesota. Only two months a state, 'spect they're strong for us, clear in their hatred of slavery."

"Still, Mr. Garrison might be right. Staying in union with slave states makes us all culpable. I'll leave you to your work. The public needs to read this."

Colin took a copy of the paper with him as they left. Once outside, Warren led them on a brisk walk to Union Street and the Union Oyster House for lunch. His son watched waiters deliver bowls of chowder and plates of fresh fish. He thought of the early mornings when he shivered at dockside unloading the night's catch and wondered if these diners had any idea some child might have had the same experience before the day's sunrise in Boston.

While Colin studied the menu, trying to discern the value of a dollar to the pounds he knew in London, his father leaned across the table and said, "Do you know who Daniel Webster was?"

"Heard the name, but no."

"A Senator from this Commonwealth of Massachusetts, and U.S. Secretary of State. He used to eat right over there, consuming six plates of oysters at a sitting. I'll tell you something else: before this was a restaurant, Louis Philippe, the exiled future king of France, fled to Boston during the French Revolution. It's said he made a living teaching the French language to women on the second floor of this very building. I suspect he educated them in more than language."

Colin smiled, looked around the room and, for the first time since their reunion, wondered if his father had a woman in his life.

"Did you enjoy meeting Ben at the printing office? Did he seem like a human being to you? You should know he's not. So says the Supreme Court of this 'free' country. Just last year, the court ruled slaves, any persons from Africa, can never be citizens, have no constitutional rights, and are merely property. Lest there be any thought of recourse, the court ruled Congress has no authority to exclude slavery or to impart freedom on slaves or non-white people. So, there's your 'land of the free and home of the brave.'"

Over lunch, his father explained that William Lloyd Garrison was the staunchest leader of the abolitionist movement.

"He created *The Liberator* in 1831; it roused so much anger in the south, Georgia's legislature passed a $5,000 reward for his capture and conveyance to that state for trial. Other states offered rewards for him, dead or alive. Mail bags containing his paper were seized and burned; gangs broke up anti-slavery gatherings. The Postmaster of the United States prohibited the paper from being delivered to the South.

"In 1834 an angry mob captured Garrison outside a meeting of Boston's Female Anti-Slavery Movement. They roped and dragged him toward Boston Commons demanding he be tarred and feathered. When the mayor was alerted, he intervened, placing Garrison under arrest and taking him to the Leverett Street Jail for his own protection."

"I thought slavery didn't exist in Massachusetts," Colin said. "Why would a mob attack Garrison in Boston?"

"The enlightened citizens of this state fear the Negro. If slavery's abolished, the Poles, the Irish, and Germans will have to compete with free blacks for their jobs. Wages might fall dramatically.

"Most abolitionists want slaves returned to Africa, don't want them living here with full rights of citizenship, don't believe them to be truly human. Even ministers preach in favor of the practice, using Bible verses to persuade their congregation slavery's a natural part of God's order. Their sermons claim Exodus, Leviticus, Luke, Colossians, all affirm it. By contrast, Mr. Garrison argues for their full equality."

Colin was impressed with Garrison's courage but worried his father could be in danger. How was this any concern of theirs?

They were together again. What purpose would it serve if his father was caught up by a mob, attacked for supporting Garrison in a hopeless fight that would never be solved by a little four-page newspaper? He read another article at the bottom of *The Liberator's* front page:

"**Republicanism of Illinois.** At a State Republican Convention in Illinois, a 'Declaration of Principals' was put forth from which we copy the following soothing assurance:

'We recognize the equal rights of all the States, and avow our readiness and willingness to maintain them, and disclaim any intention of attempting, either directly or indirectly, to assail or abridge the rights of any of the members of the Confederacy guaranteed by the Constitution, or IN ANY MANNER TO INTERFERE WITH THE INSTITUTION OF SLAVERY IN THE STATES WHERE IT EXISTS."

He showed it to his father, whose hands trembled as he read. Warren's face grew red and a vein on his neck throbbed into prominence. "And these are Republicans! Have they no backbone, no conscience?" He crumpled the paper into a tight ball and threw it on the floor.

Joseph Newton

Joseph Newton slammed the door and hurried across the room to the desk occupied by his brother Thaddeus.

"That boy's trouble. I know he is. It's only been two weeks, and Phelps is already acting as if his son will run the business. This could ruin everything."

"Relax, brother. He's young, with no experience in the affairs of business, and may have no facility for numbers. He's a temporary nuisance at best, one we can deal with in time."

"I don't like how Phelps includes him in everything. The boy's been asking me about our customers, our suppliers. As long as Warren's distracted with Garrison and slavery, I've a free hand, but if that boy is given an active part, we could be undone."

"You worry needlessly. Get him in school, introduce him to some girls. He doesn't even know where he is yet."

"Perhaps. Let me see the ledger."

Thaddeus opened the large leather-bound book on his desk and turned it so Joseph could see its columns of numbers.

"It's well disguised. Only the sharpest eyes—ones with good knowledge of accounting—could see anything amiss."

Joseph studied the numbers for a minute, then looked his brother in the eye and weakly said, "I know I worry overly much. You've always been the calm one. We continue with the plan."

"Of course we do. What have you brought me today?"

Joseph opened his briefcase and withdrew a stack of bills. "Ninety-six dollars entered as the purchase of copper. I just need one of your artistic receipts."

"And a glass of Scotch, I'll wager."

Joseph smiled, his confidence returning.

Mary Dowling

A reception was held on Beacon Street in the largest private mansion Colin had ever seen. Hosted by an industrialist and staunch abolitionist, it was an opportunity for Warren to introduce his son to a social circle to which he felt especially attached.

The room was elegantly appointed with sparkling crystal chandeliers shining brightly from high ceilings, illuminating fine oil paintings and tapestries. Velvet curtains flowed down to priceless Turkish rugs. Roman statuary near the base of the marble staircase guarded two enormous Chinese vases overflowing with flowers and greenery.

Men and women clustered in small groups, exchanging pleasantries and discussing events of the day. Colin was surprised the genders mixed so fluidly. He was more accustomed to seeing men grouped with men, and women with women.

William Lloyd Garrison sat in a high wingback chair with a group of people gathered around him. He gently pounded the armrest with his right fist, explaining the immorality of staying in union with slave-holding states, arguing the north should secede from a country ruled by so vile a Constitution. Warren wanted to introduce Colin, but clearly Garrison was in no mood for an interruption.

A woman tapped Warren's shoulder. "Ah, Mr. Phelps. So good to see you. I understand you've provided a financial lifeline to *The Liberator*. We have much to thank you for."

Warren's face brightened. "Abby Kelley, you are too kind. My contribution pales in contrast to all you've done for the cause. It is I who am in your debt, I'm quite sure. Please allow me to introduce you to my son. Mrs. Kelley, this is Colin, recently returned with me from London. Colin, Abby is a force for anti-slavery and for the rights of women. There is no hardship she hasn't endured for those causes."

Abby extended her hand, saying, "I hope we have a new young warrior for the fight."

Colin smiled uncomfortably, not sure how to respond. He took her hand and said, "It's an honor to meet you, Ma'am."

She raised her elbow with her hand pointed to the ceiling. "When I am older, you may call me Ma'am. For now, I am simply Abby. Yes?" She smiled.

"Yes," he returned her smile, quickly feeling at ease. While Abby and his father talked, Colin noticed a girl about his age delivering a silver tray of salmon to the dining room.

He caught just a glimpse, but it was enough to create a quick flutter of his heart. She was a flash of grace and beauty. He wondered if he'd really seen her properly, or if he'd just imagined what she looked like.

Abby Kelley drifted away, and his father whispered to Colin, "She's Joan of Arc in the battle for equal rights. She's been pelted with eggs, threatened with death, chased from halls, ostracized from her church.

"Several years ago, abolitionists built a grand hall in Philadelphia. It stood for only four days. Abby and Mr. Garrison each spoke there to a large crowd of whites and free blacks, men and women together. The people of that 'City of Brotherly Love' came out in force, demanding the hall be closed. Anger grew to a fever pitch and the building was set ablaze.

"The fire department arrived only to watch, not daring to sprinkle as much as a drop of water on the fire in front of fifteen-hundred angry anti-abolitionists and opponents of women's rights."

His father became engaged in a long conversation with another man, giving Colin an opportunity to explore the mansion.

He headed toward the dining room, with its broad table laden with food, surrounded by party guests filling small plates. A buffet on the side held decanters of wine and whiskey next to a row of crystal glasses. But the girl he had seen was gone.

Colin wandered down a wide hallway, passing a wood-paneled library on his left, arriving at a music room farther down. It was large enough to hold an audience of thirty. An impressive harp with intricate inlayed decorations stood by the window next to a grand piano. She wasn't here; the room was empty.

He gently ran his fingers along the strings of the harp, listening to each note, then sat on the piano bench admiring the instrument. His left hand began stroking the keys, forming a chord that slowly, gently repeated like a heartbeat. He brought the fingers of his right up over the keys and played a soft flourish, as if leaves were stirring or birds were taking flight. He melded the bass tones with the treble and pumped the floor pedal, sustaining the sound as the music took on a rich flowing melody.

The notes lifted, arched, turned, and floated down before climbing again with velvet tones, like soft fabric flowing in the wind. He let the notes subside, slowly rocking forward, bending toward the keyboard with his forehead over the keys. Another flourish, and a gentle sustained dying of the notes. He sat for a second, straightening his back, admiring the instrument, when he heard two hands clapping behind him.

Colin turned to see her standing in the doorway, her hands on her hips. The girl he'd glimpsed earlier.

"So, we've a musician amongst us. Tell me, though, there's no sheet music. Where did y' learn that piece?"

Her eyes were filled with mischief and excitement. Dark hair falling to her shoulders, framing her smiling face, tied by a bright blue ribbon that matched her eyes. He felt nervous, turning on the bench to face her and blushing a bit, wondering if he was in trouble for playing the piano. "Perhaps I shouldn't be here."

"It's of no consequence ta me, but I think a piano's in need o' play'n' every now and again. Where'd ya learn that piece? 'Twas lovely."

"It's just something from my head. I sometimes create music in my mind."

"And that's in yer mind? It's some kind of head you've got there. Does yer song have a name?"

"I call it America."

"Is that so?" she laughed. "Well, you've a high opinion o' this place, judge'n' by yer tune."

"I've not been here long. It's just impressions I played. Perhaps if I knew the country better ..."

"Well by then, you'll be play'n' a different tune all together, I'd wager."

"You're Irish, I assume. I'm from London, and this country's still a mystery to me half the time."

"If you don't mind me say'n', you'll find an easier time here being from England than anyone from Ireland ever has."

"Is that a fact? Perhaps if I knew the country, I would play a different melody. Maybe you could show me more of Boston ... possibly on Saturday?"

"And ya presume I've noth'n' better ta do?"

"I presume I couldn't find a better guide." He stood, smiled, and gave a slight bow. "I'm Colin. My father's Warren Phelps. I've only been here a few weeks. Not meaning to presume, but if you have a free day. I barely know a soul here, so you would do me a great service. May I ask your name?"

"Mary Dowling. Been employed in this household fer two years and have had little time to explore the city m'self. Perhaps one o' m' five brothers could give you a tour."

"I'd much prefer your perspective."

"I'm sure you would, but Irish servants and British gents are hardly compatible, especially in America."

She moved toward the harp. Her trim figure and lithe movements gave the impression of a dancer. He thought she moved with the efficiency and grace of a ballerina. Mary plucked a few strings on the harp, eyeing him playfully.

"And I suppose you'd want to bring me flowers and have a picnic on the Commons and stroll along the Charles River."

Colin, flustered, said, "I would only ask that you show me what you like of the city, and help me know what to avoid. Do you have a free day? A few hours?"

She ran the back of her thumbnail along the harp strings and said, "If ya play yer song again, I might find a suitable time." Mary motioned toward the piano, and he returned to the bench.

Colin played the same composition, note for note, while Mary studied the movements of his fingers. The music began drawing guests from the party. They stood quietly behind him, listening to him play, turning to one another with approving nods of their heads. His father was among those who gathered. Warren had had no idea his son could play; the revelation fascinated him.

A Bargain Is Struck

Joseph Newton sat in his small office at the rear of the factory floor. He held a contract in his left hand, a fountain pen in his right. He laid the pen down on the desk and stared across at a bald man with a precisely trimmed dark beard and expensive suit.

"You've supplied our firm for two years, and your components have been quite satisfactory. However, you have competitors now. Just this week, I was approached by someone who offered to supply the very same product for a significant reduction in price."

The salesman sat up and leaned across the desk. "I'm sure it's an inferior product, and I'm certain you would suffer delivery delays." He extended two fingers, tapping the desk as he spoke, "No need to invite uncertainty when you know the quality of our product."

"That may be so, but I've an obligation to improve profits for Mr. Phelps. The price of goods must be monitored closely, and often." He opened a tobacco pouch and began filling the bowl of his pipe. "It's an obligation that places constant strain upon me, as you can imagine. Perhaps you might suggest a way of reducing that burden. After all, the less I am burdened, the more useful I can be to my employer."

"You've been a good and constant customer, Mr. Newton. Is there something you might want to propose?"

"I might be persuaded to renew your contract, in all its current terms mind you, if I had assurance you would refund to me personally one dollar for every twenty-five dollars we spend with you."

Newton struck a match and drew the flame into his pipe.

The man sat back in his chair for a moment, then stroked his beard before slowly saying, "I believe that is a reasonable request, given the circumstances."

Newton pointed the stem of his pipe at the man. "To me personally."

"I understand."

He picked up the pen and said, "This is a matter to be held in the strictest of confidence, and a matter not to be defaulted on. Not even once."

A nod of the head confirmed the agreement, and the contract was signed.

Newton smiled as he shook the gentleman's hand and escorted him to the door.

City Tour

She had agreed to show him a bit of Boston. Sunday was her day off, and only after church. He met her there at the base of the steps, surprised to see her escorted out by three other men. Two were older, and one was slightly younger. He hesitated to approach.

Mary smiled. "Some of me brothers were eager to meet ya. Allow me to introduce Michael, Brendan, and Brian."

The oldest, Michael, looked to be in his early twenties, tall, muscular, and confident. He moved down the stairs surveying Colin, looking him up and down, before extending his hand and saying, "You'll have her home by supper, then?"

"I will."

She had changed her hairstyle, wearing ringlets that bounced as she walked. He wanted to reach up and take her arm as she descended but worried her brothers might take offense. Instead, he clasped his hands in front of him, like a groom awaiting his bride.

Mary stood next to him with her back to the church, arched her head toward her brothers and said, "They're not about ta bite ya. Not yet at least. This way."

She walked off briskly. Colin needed a quick turn and a rapid pace to catch up.

"Hey! Where're we going?"

"First off, you're treat'n' me to a decent meal at The Green Dragon, and then I'll be showing ya a thing or two about Irish tradition."

"Is that a fact?"

"Tis a fact indeed." A satisfied smile.

He had to nearly double his pace to keep up.

The restaurant was filling fast. They got the last open table. Mary pointed to the sign proclaiming the tavern as "The Headquarters of the Revolution."

"Ya said you did nae know the country well. I thought you'd like to see where America began. The Boston Tea Party was planned here. John Hancock's brother lived next door. The two of them were in here all the time, thick as thieves; so was Paul Revere."

"I've heard of Hancock. Who was Paul Revere?"

She laughed. "Ya really don't know much about America yet, do ya? If you want yer pretty music to reflect this land, you've got to know her better."

He leaned forward resting his elbow on the table, two fingers out beckoning her to continue. "I'm all ears."

She relayed what she could remember, and what she'd been told, much of which bore no resemblance to the truth. He was captivated by her easy spirit and confidence. Mary's sense of humor was cutting and self-deprecating at the same time. Mostly, she liked to point out the absurdities of life, its inconsistencies. He watched the freckles across her nose as she talked, almost afraid to look into the sparkle and energy of her eyes.

Colin was relieved she carried the weight of the conversation, feeling nervous and self-conscious, filling each silence with questions so he wouldn't say anything that might betray his ignorance.

Mary ordered only a cup of chowder, while Colin favored shepherd's pie. "Is that all you're eating?"

"I prefer to be light on me feet. Hurry with yer stew, we've someplace to be."

He gave her a questioning look. "And where might that be?"

"You'll see soon enough." She held her arm out, rolling her hand in a circular motion to indicate he should speed up. "It wouldn't do t' be late."

He took two quick last bites, pushed his plate aside, turned, and signaled to their waiter for the check.

Outside, she walked with brisk powerful strides, forcing him nearly into a run to catch up. Mary led him on a circuitous route, taking shortcuts through alleyways, and even walking in one door of a dress shop and out the back to shorten their route. Her final destination was an Irish pub, the Angel's Harp.

When she burst through the door, several gentlemen smiled, acknowledging her; some even stood to greet her.

"Mary, we've missed ya! Good seeing ya again, lass."

She smiled, giving a short wave and a few quick words as she breezed past them to the back room. Colin followed cautiously, eyeing the men at the bar.

Four girls waited for her in the large open room. They converged on Mary, giggling and hugging her as she walked through the door. They were dressed in short Irish dance costumes. Two wore thick black tap shoes, and two wore soft black slippers laced from toes to ankles.

Mary smiled, "Ah, m' darlings. Are the others here yet?"

"On their way, no doubt," said the tallest girl, "and I'm sure they're look'n' fer the prize."

Mary laughed, "They'll soon find they've no chance. Not against my girls."

Colin looked baffled.

"It's a feis," she explained. "A competition. Every Sunday, we compete with dancers from other neighborhoods. We've held the lead so far, but tonight'll be a fight, fer sure. Stay at the bar while I get ready. You may see a face or two you know."

Colin couldn't imagine who she meant but turned and walked back into the pub's main room. He'd been there less than ten minutes when Mary's brothers breezed through the door.

"Well, if it isn't the English lad!" Michael said. "Our gratitude to ya for chaperoning her. I'm sure Mary would want you to buy us some pints."

Colin's father had given him money for the week. It wasn't likely to outlast the night. The drinks were poured, and Michael said, "Cheap piss compared to beer in the Old Country, but ya get used to it after a while."

Colin smiled weakly.

Musicians arrived, a tall thin fiddler accompanied by an older pot-bellied bearded man with a mandolin, a woman with auburn hair carrying a flute, and a boy, not much older than fourteen, with a drum. They set up in the back room and began tuning their instruments.

Customers shuffled into the back, taking seats facing a small wooden stage. Additional gas lights were lit, and more chairs were moved into place. Michael and his brothers sauntered into the back room with Colin in tow. A rustle of conversation erupted from the front room. The dancers from the other neighborhood were arriving. Some men whistled, others tossed out discouraging comments and crude remarks.

Michael signaled the waitress, his hand in the air pointing at Colin and his brothers in a circular motion. She understood and left to pour another round. The crowd settled down as Mary climbed onto the stage.

She'd changed into a traditional Irish dancing costume. A ribbon of flowers was woven through the ringlets of her hair. She wore a short dress, flared at the waist, with bright embroidery of blue, white, and green, trimmed at the bottom with a strip of lace. Her black stockings matched the color of her soft dancing shoes.

"Tis the pleasure of the Angel's Harp, and our neighborhood, to welcome the girls from Dorchester. We've heard fine accounts of their performances this year and will respect them as worthy opponents. By that I mean, we'll try not to make 'em cry." She teased with a mischievous grin that was met with a roaring round of laughter and applause.

"As our guests, they've the floor first." Mary waved over the platform, indicating it was theirs.

Two girls walked to center stage and stood erect, awaiting the music. The drum began a rhythmic beat. The girls retained stiff upper bodies, while lifting off the stage, coming down with a firm click. The tapping of their shoes matched the beating of the drum as the dancers crossed their ankles, turned, and lifted again.

The fiddle struck up a lively pace, and the flute and mandolin joined in. The girls turned, each bending one knee and lifting it high behind their other leg, then striking the stage again, their taps perfectly matching the music. Their movements were swift and energetic, picking up steam as the music sped up. Colin was impressed, excited by the music, the dancers, and the beer. He tapped his foot with the beat and smiled.

When the dance ended to enthusiastic applause, it was time for two of Mary's girls to perform. The music was the same, and the dancers began in much the same fashion as the prior two, but their energy and enthusiasm grew, as did their smiles, when they realized they were taking control of the floor. The applause greeting their performance was far more boisterous than the one their competitors had received.

The next two sets were danced by girls in soft shoes. There was no tapping; rather, their intricate moves expressed grace and power. Again, the audience was more disposed to the home team.

Colin wondered why Mary hadn't danced with any of them. He decided she was their coach and, despite her costume, not a participant. She stood at the far end of the stage applauding the previous dancers. A brief silence after the ovation was followed by the drum again. It struck a strong, forceful clip.

Mary gave a short skip, then thrust her right leg high into the air and sailed across the stage like a deer clearing a fence. Her soft landing was followed by quick movements as her feet crossed rapidly front to back, while her torso remained erect, her hands on her hips. A quick jump as she kicked her leg high in front of her was followed by swift footwork, swirls, and smiles.

The music grew faster, almost a frenzy; she matched it with confidence. Many of the men in the room stood, clapping their hands in time with the beat, cheering her on. Colin had never seen anything as captivating and lively.

It was official: he was falling for her. Mary's performance ended to an enthusiastic ovation. She held her arms out wide, bowed at the waist, and repeated the bow when the crowd cheered louder. She skipped off the stage with a triumphant grin. There was little question as to which team would be awarded the ribbon that day.

While they waited for her to change, Michael ordered another round. Colin calculated how many dollars he might still have in his wallet, and how much more of his sobriety could be spared.

Mary joined them, beaming with her victory and happy to see everyone getting along so well. "What did ya think?"

"It was a marvel," Colin said. "You were spectacular."

"A bit different from the slow, cow-like dances you see on English floors, is it not?"

Colin thought of the sedate, sluggishly polite quality of dancers he'd seen only once at a banker's affair his father took him to during his last week in London. He had to admit it held none of the fun and energy that he'd just witnessed.

"As different as anything I could imagine."

"Now yer learn'n a thing or two about us Irish. Do ya know why we hold our upper body so erect? In the old days there were no dance floors. Contests were held on the top of a barrel. It was all feet and balance."

Michael turned to Colin, gave him a friendly slap on the shoulder, and said, "No need to walk her home. We'll take her from here."

She gave him a shrug, a wink, and an impish grin. He watched them all walk out.

A House Divided

Warren folded the *Boston Herald*, laying it on the table beside him. Ever since last year's Dred Scott decision, everything seemed lost. The court's ruling was clear. Slaves could never be citizens, would never have constitutional rights, and furthermore, the Constitution protected slavery from any interference by Congress. He despaired for the nation, and he gave serious thought to taking Colin, packing up, and returning to England. But he had made a solemn oath to God.

After causing the death of Captain Winters, he had resolved to seek absolution. His sin wasn't only the taking of a life; he recalled the faces of the slaves he had helped capture from Cuba. He remembered seeing them auctioned like stacks of wood or cattle.

Back in Hatteras, in his little room in the parsonage, he'd gotten on to his knees, cried, and begged the Lord for forgiveness. He pledged he would spend his life fighting to bring about the end of slavery in America.

At that time, he thought his promise would include a life with Dottie at his side. Returning to find her buried and Colin gone, he knew this was retribution for his sins. Rather than turning away from his pledge, he accepted the judgment of God and redoubled efforts to make restitution, to save his soul.

Now the Dred Scott decision had closed the doors on abolition. The newspaper further reported on Republican debates in Illinois. A little-known former congressman, Abraham Lincoln, had given a series of speeches stressing the biblical admonition, "A house divided against itself cannot stand."

Lincoln argued the nation would not be dissolved, but it would cease to be divided. "It will become all one thing, or all the other." Slavery would be outlawed, or it would spread across the entire country. Slavery was not just an economic issue to Lincoln; it was a matter of highest moral and political importance. So went his debates with Stephen Douglas.

Warren was encouraged by the language, but the Republican Party at its convention in Chicago had made it clear their platform in no way meant to interfere with southern slave-holding states. Well, he thought, the Republicans are as weak as most northerners. Besides, Lincoln is an inconsequential figure, likely to lose his Senate race.

He looked up when Colin came home. The boy breezed into the room announcing newfound admiration for America and its possibilities. He smiled and swayed a step backwards, saying, "Did you know Irish girls danced on barrels?"

Warren rose and placed his hands on Colin's arm, guiding him to the sofa.

"So, you've been drinking alcohol and watching girls dance?" He crossed his arms across his chest, staring down at the boy.

"It's not like that, father." Slurring his words. "I enjoyed a perfectly civil meal with a girl I met at the reception last week. I joined her after church, and she told me stories of America's history. She took me to watch her feis, an Irish dance contest. Very colorful and exuberant!" He brought both hands in front of him and snapped his fingers. "Such energy!"

"You met an Irish girl at a Catholic church and thought it would be appropriate to go to a pub, where you've obviously been drinking, and she's a dancer?"

Colin looked up with a broad grin on his face. "Yes! It was delightful." He tried to stand but fell back onto the couch.

"You need to go to bed. We'll discuss this in the morning. And I will find ways to introduce you to some proper girls. The Irish are fickle, uneducated, and overly fond of drink. I've failed in not pointing that out to you."

Colin was surprised at his father's tone. He started to say something but thought better of it. He grasped the arm of the sofa with both hands, pulled himself up, and headed for the stairs.

An Education

The next morning, Warren shook Colin awake, handing him a cup of tea. His son sat up, rubbing his eyes, and stifling a yawn. He blinked.

"It's early. The sun's not up yet."

"We've waited too long to get you in a proper school. It's time we remedy that. Get dressed; we've a busy day ahead."

Colin planted his feet on the floor, his head feeling the fuzzy effects of too many pints the previous night. Nevertheless, his father's tone motivated him to hurry.

At the bottom of the stairs, his father tossed him an orange. "You can eat this on the way."

They walked along nearly vacant streets without speaking. Colin looked at his father twice, but the man's forceful stride, with his jaw set, conveyed he was on a mission, in no mood to talk. Colin peeled the orange, collecting his thoughts.

"I meant no harm yesterday. She's a good girl. Three of her brothers were with us the whole time, and her dancing was a contest of skills against another neighborhood. She's worked at the Worthington's mansion for two years. I'm sure they'll attest to her reputation."

"She's Irish. You haven't been here long enough to know certain things. The Irish can be shiftless, inviting trouble, with a tendency toward drunkenness and thievery. They're fine amongst themselves, but I've not brought you from London to see you so distracted. I've enjoyed being with you so much I've neglected your education."

"I can learn machinery crafts, work in your factory."

"There's time enough for that. I want you prepared for a broader life than the factory offers. You've a higher calling."

Colin tossed the last of his orange peel into the alley. He folded his arms in front of his chest, stared down at the street, and kicked a stone to the side. "My calling is to be with you. It's what mother would have wanted."

"She'd want you to have a better life. One full of blessings and success. She'd want me to keep you from going astray. That girl's an impediment for you."

Colin glared at his father, shoved his hands into his pockets, seething in silence.

They reached the factory, and Warren led his son along the assembly floor to Joseph Newton's office in the back. Newton wasn't there. Warren looked around, spread his arms wide as he turned searching the whole of the factory. "He's meant to be here early on Mondays. Sit here and wait for him. I'll be back."

Colin sat in the small wooden chair across from the desk. He studied the room. Newton had added some refinements, a Turkish rug on the floor, a map of Boston on one wall, a painting of a clipper ship on the other. His desktop was precisely arranged. A tobacco pouch rested against a pipe rack designed for three pipes, but only holding two. Newton must have the other one with him. An expensive fountain pen set with a marble base and a crystal inkwell added a touch of elegance, as did a gold letter opener with a carved ivory handle.

As the time ticked by, Colin grew restless. He stood and went around to the front of the desk, letting two of his fingers slide along the surface, realizing it was completely clean. None of the dust and debris from the factory floor settled on it, or it had been fastidiously polished. Newton, it seemed, was compulsive.

He looked down at the drawers, then up through the door and the window that looked out onto the assembly floor. Still no sign of Newton. Colin slid the center drawer open: pencils in separate groups held by rubber bands, pipe cleaners, two fountain pens. Nothing exciting.

He closed it and opened another drawer. It held a stack of invoices and receipts. The next drawer held two green bound ledgers. The bottom drawer held a bottle of whiskey and a small metal box. Colin tried it, but the box was locked. He also found a paper with his father's signature repeated over and over. He was about to take it out when he heard conversation from the factory floor. Newton was striding toward his office. Colin slid the drawer closed with his leg, then turned to look at the map.

"Studying Boston?"

"Still getting my bearings."

"It takes a while, but you'll learn soon enough. I've spoken with your father. He wants me to get you enrolled. So, we'll head out soon. I've a friend at Boston Latin who should be of help to us."

"What kind of school is that? I've little knowledge of Latin."

"It's the oldest public school in America. Five signers of the Declaration of Independence went there. Benjamin Franklin attended but dropped out. It's really the only school to consider."

It turned out, however, that Boston Latin wouldn't consider Colin. "No proper foundation," they said. Furthermore, his age of nearly seventeen would afford little time to salvage his education. Colin was secretly happy.

Shopping for A Friend

The schooling of young master Phelps was put on hold for the time being. He spent his days in the factory, helping where he could, learning from the various skilled mechanics. He enjoyed the activity, the energy, and the sense of helping his father.

There was still the issue of the Irish girl. His father didn't address it directly but made a few mumbled references to the unreliability of "those people."

On Wednesday afternoon, Colin slipped away and walked to Beacon Street. He stood outside the Worthington mansion, hoping to catch a glimpse of her, walking back and forth in front of the house, thinking if he passed more windows, she'd have a better chance of spotting him. If she did, there was no sign of it. He finally gave up, shoved his hands into his pockets, and walked home.

Friday morning, a delivery boy arrived at the factory looking for Mr. Phelps.

"I'll take that," Colin said, without looking up, still fixing his attention on a screw he was turning. He reached out his hand for the envelope, but it was tugged out of his grasp at the last second. "Well, if 't isn't the fine English gentleman."

Colin straightened to discover Brendan Dowling, Mary's brother.

"Brendan! I didn't know it was you. What's this?" Taking the envelope back.

"Don't know. Never do. Is this your dad's business, then?" He looked around, taking in the size of the factory; obviously impressed.

"It is, Brendan. How's the family?"

"If you mean Mary, she's do'n' quite well."

"Has she mentioned me?"

"All the time. Can't talk o' anyone else," He replied with a bright twinkle and a laugh.

"Seriously."

"She said you were nice. Said you were a bit awkward too. Michael and I are go'n' out t'night. Maybe you'd like to come. Mary might be there. You could buy us a round." He looked around the factory again, "or two."

Colin barely heard him. *Awkward? How was I awkward?* he wondered.

"So, ya com'n' tonight?"

He looked toward his father's office but knew he was at *The Liberator*, as he was every Friday.

"What time? Where will you be?"

"Could be anywhere but most likely at Flanagan's. Do you know it?"

"No. What's it near?"

"Meet us at the Angel's Harp at six o'clock. Michael has some shopping to do."

"Done. See you at 6." He reached out to shake hands, but Brendan gave him a quick salute instead. "6, then."

That evening Colin left a note for his father saying he was meeting a friend for supper, and he'd be home at a reasonable hour. He also wrote a few lines describing how the business day had gone.

His heart floated with expectation as he hurried to the pub. If she thought him awkward, he'd do his best to be smooth and confident. He arrived ten minutes early and waited at the bar, sipping tea.

Brendan and Michael burst through the door with a third person who they introduced as Tom Casey. Tom was handsome and funny with a strong sense of himself. Mary was nowhere in sight. He would have asked if she was coming but didn't want to sound too eager, still not sure what her brothers thought of him.

"I believe you promised us a pint." Brendan slapped Colin on the back and received a resigned shrug in return. He signaled the bartender and held up four fingers.

While they drank, Michael explained Tom had a special date that night with a woman who'd won his heart. He worried he had only his work clothes, and not a decent jacket to wear.

They were about to go shopping for him. Colin paid the tab, and they headed out.

Instead of going to a clothing store, they went directly to Flanagan's Public House. On the way, Brendan confided to Colin that Mary might join them there. It was enough to wangle another set of drafts from Colin.

They sat at a table near the door. Michael and his friend spent little time talking, instead focusing their attention on each person who entered. About fifteen minutes into it, Michael tapped Tom's arm and turned his head toward two men who just arrived. Tom looked at them, smiled, and nodded his approval.

"Check the size," Michael said in a low voice. The two men were standing at the bar. Tom went and stood behind them for a minute. He turned to Michael and subtly indicated the man on the right. Michael smiled, getting up from the table.

He approached the men and engaged the one on the right, asking where he was from. Wasn't he the one who had insulted his family? The man gave him an incredulous look. He swore he'd never seen Michael and had no idea who his family happened to be. Michael grew more aggressive and hostile, hurling insults at the man. It was clear a fight was brewing.

"You've some nerve act'n' as if ya di'nae know what ya did to m' sister."

"I've not the least idea who you mean, but if her face is anything like yours, you can be sure I'd have nothing to do with her."

"Ya great big ape of a man, if there's any face th' needs correct'n', it's yers."

The men moved away from the bar, circling each other, matching insult for insult as patrons began gathering round. Michael put up his fists to strike but hesitated. He held his hands up in a stop position. "Wouldn't want yer blood all over me fine jacket." He took it off and handed it to Tom. The other man gave a slight shrug, removed his jacket, and also entrusted it to Tom.

Michael threw the first blow, partially blocked by his foe. The crowd yelled instructions, guiding the movements of the fight.

With everyone's attention riveted on the combatants, Tom edged backwards through the cheering patrons, turned toward Brendan and Colin, and cocked his head toward the door. They all scampered out, running around the corner down to the end of the block. Tom gave Michael's jacket to Brendan before trying the new one on. "A perfect fit," he smiled. "Tell him I am in his debt." A quick wave, and he was gone.

Colin looked at Brendan. "Should we help your brother?"

Brendan laughed, "He's in no need o' help. Come on."

They retraced their steps to The Angel's Harp. Colin was still feeling adrenaline from the excitement. He slapped Brendan on the shoulder. "I think it's your turn to buy."

Ten minutes later, Michael sauntered in without a scratch on him. "Where were we then?" Brendan smiled and handed him a shot of whiskey.

Colin missed some of the bragging and storytelling, keeping an eye out for Mary, glancing frequently at the door.

"Did you say Mary will be here?"

Brendan broke off his conversation, turning toward Colin with a beer nearly to his lips. He hesitated, lowered the glass, and said, "Why do ya think Thomas needed a fine new jacket? Did I nae tell ya he had a date with a girl this evening?"

Colin stiffened, clenched his fists, and stared directly into Brendan's eyes. "Mary and Thomas?"

Brendan burst out laughing. "Heavens no! I wouldn't let the scoundrel anywhere near her. Just hav'n' some fun. Here, I've got someth'n' fer ya." He pulled an envelope out of his pocket and handed it over. "From Mary."

Colin opened it, turning away to read it to himself:

If it's another tour you're need'n', I can meet 5:30 Saturday evening at the church, but I won't wait a minute beyond that." He smiled, folding the note, slipping it into his pocket, and gently tapping it with his hand.

Brendan chuckled. "Ya know there's a beer tax for deliver'n' letters. It's usually two rounds, but I'll let ya off w' only one." Colin was happy to oblige.

Benedictus Smith

Colin slept until 9:00 Saturday morning. He had promised his father to spend the day at *The Liberator*. With Friday's edition put to bed, Saturdays were devoted to cleaning the press, organizing the office, and taking inventory of supplies.

Benedictus was already hard at work, humming as he swept the floor. Colin stood in the doorway, watching him from behind, intimidated by the large Negro. "Chariots," Ben sang out, and returned to humming as the broom moved in time with the beat.

Colin tapped cautiously on the door frame. Ben swirled around, staring at the boy before realizing who he was, then crossed his muscular arms in front of his chest and smiled.

"Now here's a sight. I 'spect you come to learn more o' your daddy's passion. How can Benedictus Smith be o' help to you, young'un?"

"Promised my father I'd come help you with your chores."

"Now, dat's someth'n' fo' the ages. A fine English gentleman help'n' da likes o' me. You are indeed your daddy's son."

"I can help you clean, get things in proper order, and perhaps, you can teach me something of the printing trade?"

"A bargain well-struck. I cain't be print'n' forever. Could use a hand." He picked up a broom leaning against the counter and handed it to Colin.

"First the floor, next we clean our press, sort the typeset, and restock. Afterwards, I be pleased to show you how de press works. You ever printed afore?"

"No. Is it complicated?"

"Easy anuf, if you's careful. One step at a time. Life by the yard is hard, life by the inch is a cinch." He laughed at himself and reached out with his large fist, tapping Colin on the shoulder.

Colin swept quietly for a few minutes, unsure of how to talk with this large bear of a man.

"How'd you learn the trade?"

Ben was wiping the press with a rag soaked in solvent.

"Your father hasn't told you?"

"No. Did you go to school?"

"Let's just say I've an education few could match, and none would want."

"Where did you …?"

"Not Boston. Hopewell, Virginia. On a large tobacco farm owned by Mr. Oliver Enders, a dull, arrogant beast who thought he was do'n' God's work by keep'n' his slaves clothed in rags, fed with scraps, and beaten into submission."

"You were a slave?"

"Still am, if they catch me. Ol' Massa Enders was head o' the county militia. He and the fine church folk loved noth'n' better an to take their weekly rides, inspect'n' farms, searching for runaways. Loved ta put God's discipline into the heart and hide o' every Negro they could."

"You're a runaway?"

"I was eighteen. My mother died in the heat of the field. She sank to a knee, and Enders lashed her with a whip. She fell hard, and my brother went to take the whip from him. Pulled it right outa his hand. Be'n' a God-fearing man, Enders took the shotgun off his saddle and blew Daniel's head away. He looked at me and said, 'I've another shell in here if you want it.' He clubbed my mother with the butt end, and she was gone. I was too afraid to move. But I vowed he'd never get another day o' work out a me. And he never did.

"Took off dat night but didn't go north. They'd be look'n' there. No, sir, I went straight south down the James River. From the time I was a baby they told us stories of alligators and flesh-eat'n' fish liv'n' all up and down the James. Let'n' em eat me was better than what Enders woulda did, and I wouldn't give him the satisfaction. I held my breath and waded in. Hid among the marshes by daylight, then clung to a log by night, floating south for four nights, dodging man and beast till I got clear down to the Chesapeake Bay.

"Spent two days off Norfolk, watch'n' the ships, live'n' on what clams and oysters I could dig, wait'n' fer a chance. Just afore day-break, a barge loaded with tobacco and cotton began head'n' slowly north. I could run faster an it was move'n' and ducked into the water a hundred yards ahead o' her to wait. She pulled so close I hardly needed to swim. Buried myself in her cargo and must've slept ten hours."

"You weren't discovered?"

"Just past Baltimore, a Quaker who worked the barge found me. Brought me food and heped me slip into the harbor with instructions on how to find a Quaker meeting house. That's where I found Nelva and John Culbertson. Two saints.

"I tapped their door like I's told, and she pulled me inside, look'n' both ways to see if we noticed. John's an Elder with the Quakers, and Nelva runs a small school. Together, they're a link in the Underground. Sent many a slave to freedom.

"Took a fever most as soon as I walked through their door. Too much time in dat river. She nursed me to health; said I should stay till I had skills enough to get by on.

"Nelva Culbertson taught me to read. Morn'n' and night, she'd practice me with letters and read the Bible till, bit by bit, I got to read'n' it to her. Then she ran me through spelling contests. I can spell 'prodigious' and 'Pentecost' and 'patience.' Can work grammar backwards and forwards.

"Mostly, she taught me about patience, waiting on God in silence, and realizing I can't change the past, but I command a powerful force over the future. We read the Declaration of Independence, where I learned I was equal, and the Constitution, where I learned I wasn't. Patience, patience. I'll be teach'n' my own children to read soon."

"You have children?"

"Boy an' a girl, Noah and Sarah. Five and four years old. A person don't know how much he can love 'til he has children o' his own. Your daddy has an affection for you you'll never understand without a child o' your own. The place you have in your poppa's heart is sacred, immovable."

"Your wife?"

"Rebecca. Stole my heart, and I stole her away from Baltimore."

"Was she a slave?"

"No, a free woman, seamstress, who risked a life with me."

"And you learned to print ...?"

"John Culbertson printed a Quaker pamphlet twice a month. He taught me to work the press, how to load each letter, run practice sheets, and check the grammar. He was strict, no mistakes allowed. I learned to do it right."

* * *

When Colin got home in the early afternoon, his father and Newton were discussing business. He didn't want to interrupt but felt compelled to tell them everything he'd learned about Ben. Much of it his father already knew, but Newton took a keen interest and made a note at the bottom of his ledger: HOPEWELL, VIRGINIA, OLIVER ENDERS.

Bell Tower

Just before 5:30, Colin bounded up the steps of Holy Cross Cathedral and paced in front of its tall wooden doors. He took out her note and read it again, confirming the place and time. He'd just slipped it back into his pocket when he saw her crossing Franklin Street. *Act calm*, he thought.

"It's an interesting group of brothers you have."

"Ya don't know the half of it. Did they drink their way through yer wallet?"

"In a manner of speaking. Where're we headed?"

"Inside."

"The church?"

"Ya want to see the city don't ya?" She grabbed his hand, leading him through the door.

"If you're thinking of converting me, it's a bit premature."

"You want to see Boston, no?" In a hushed tone, as she raised a finger to her mouth. "This way."

She led him around a side altar at the rear of the church and put a finger to her lips as she glanced around. Mary opened a narrow wooden door, revealing a set of steps. "Up here." With a slight giggle.

They climbed what seemed to be a hundred steps to the top of the bell tower, disturbing pigeons into flight.

"You were want'n' to see Boston. Well, here she is, all laid out pretty fer ya."

Mary was right. At this height, all of Boston was laid out before them. From the harbor to the Charles River, the city bustled below. Colin stared out at the tall masts of the clipper ships at port. She stood behind him, placing her hands on his shoulders and turning him around.

"There," she pointed to the gold dome of the State House. "That's Beacon Hill. You can almost see the Worthingtons' home from here. The copper roof on the State House? It was laid by Paul Revere's company. Ya remember: the patriot whose name ya d' nae know?"

She pointed across the Charles River. "That's Cambridge, and just over that way is Charlestown. You're nae afraid of heights are ya?" Mary drew him closer to the edge.

"There's little I'm afraid of … except you!" He laughed, extending a finger and touching the tip of her nose.

"Well, that ya should be, fer certain."

He turned his attention to the busy street. Two boys were chasing a wagon, intent on grabbing fruit from off its back. A scruffy dog trailed behind them, yelping. Carriages were out in number, and the sidewalks were full of pedestrians: women with shawls and pretty parasols, couples, arm-in-arm heading for dinner or a theater, newsboys hawking their papers, and lamp lighters beginning their rounds.

Colin stepped back and watched her as she peered over the side. He realized that, for the first time, Boston was beginning to feel comfortable, a bit like home.

"Come look," she urged, pointing to the street. "There's a rhythm to the city, a dance ya should capture for yer music. Tis chaos and freedom, and a hunger fer life. There's a tune for ya."

He watched the ebb and flow of the city below, realizing she was right, forming notes and melodies in his mind, tapping his foot, and nodding his head. They stood silent for a long time, taking it all in.

She turned to him anxiously, "What's the time?"

"Time?"

Mary grabbed his arm and guided him to the staircase, laughing as she led him quickly down the first several steps.

The loud clanging of the bell echoed and bounced off the narrow walls. They pressed their palms against their ears and hurried their descent. At the bottom, he bent over with his hands on his knees, breathing hard. She slapped him on the back. "Yer in fine shape, I see. Do ya never exercise?"

"Well, I'm not a dancer, if that's what you mean. I suppose I've neglected my athletics of late."

"Too much drink'n' with me brothers will do that to ya. Did ya like the view?"

He placed his hands on each side of her head and looked into her mischievous eyes. "It's a beautiful view, one I'll never forget."

"And why am I doubt'n' that?" She put her hand on his chest and a gave a gentle push. "You need to be head'n' home now. I've someplace to be."

"I'll walk you home."

"It's not to home I'm headed. I've a few chores, and I'm quite capable of handl'n' 'em on me own."

"I thought we might have supper."

"Not tonight. I haven't the time."

"Next Saturday then? Can I see you again?"

***

Colin learned the symphony played evening performances on the Commons and asked if she'd meet him Saturday for an early meal and a concert. He waited for Mary outside her employer's home and smiled as he handed her a rose.

"And here I was hop'n' fer a bouquet of four-leaf clovers. Well, a rose 'll have to do, if it's all you've brought." He was taken aback. She laughed and poked his arm. "You're a fine gentleman. I shouldn't make light of the gesture."

Mary placed her arm around his, and he smiled as they headed toward the restaurant. Colin was determined not to be awkward, but this woman kept him on edge. Conversation flowed more smoothly than on their first outing. He talked about his time at St. Anne's and his experience sailing from London. She had been on a similar voyage but was only eleven at the time. She asked him about the church choir, which Colin admitted he missed. Music held a special place for him, as it did for her.

They hurried through dinner to be early enough to get a good spot on the lawn. The orchestra was warming up. The vibration of the instruments, the yearning of the strings, and the playfulness of the horns excited him. He nudged her, pointing to the conductor. "They say he's from London too." She smiled, and for a second, he forgot the music, not knowing anything but the magic of her eyes.

Mary turned toward the musicians, and he studied her for several seconds before turning his attention back to the stage. When the concert started, he sat with his knees up, cradling them with his arms, listening to every note. He studied the pattern of the overture, watched the movements of the cellists and violinists. His fingers tapped and drummed as if playing a piano in the air.

He was capturing and memorizing entire sections of the performance. The second piece was a Mozart horn concerto.

Colin had never heard French horns played so beautifully. He sat upright, closed his eyes, and absorbed the sound.

A breeze blew in from the harbor, skidding across the Commons. Mary leaned into Colin, nestling her head on his shoulders. He wrapped an arm around her and could feel the gentle rising and falling of her rib cage as she breathed. The music began to fade from his mind.

They stood applauding when the concert ended.

"Did ya find some new notes fer that American song of yers?"

He grinned, and said, "I'm starting a whole new song. It's called Mary Dowling."

She blushed a bit, then reached up, knocking the hat off his head. "Don't be flirt'n' with me. I've someplace else to show ya." He reached for her hand, but she brushed him back, bowing her head a bit.

Thirty minutes later, they stood in a squalid part of the city across from tenement buildings with clothes hanging from each balcony, smoke streaming from small coal fires in metal barrels, goats tied in a small dirt alley, and rubbish blowing along the street. Halfway down the block a small boy urinated against a sagging wooden fence.

"So, this is what you wanted me to see?" He fidgeted, shifting from foot to foot as if eager to depart.

"Tis someth'n' ya should know." Pointing to the second balcony. "That's me home. It's where we all live. About as far from the Worthingtons' mansion as possible. If you've an idea that I'm of your social class, here's your proof to the contrary. You've had yer tour, and now you know the truth. Now, you've a new chorus for that music of yours."

"Mary, where do you think I grew up? It was on the streets till I was taken in as a charity case. I'd no education until nearly twelve and needed to fight every day to survive. Do you think I care what your home looks like? If this is supposed to discourage me, it's failing."

"Nevertheless, it's who I am. You've your place, and I've mine, if I can keep it. You mustn't see me again. It's trouble for me. I'll be go'n' in now. Can ya find yer way home?"

He watched her cross the street, moving like a dancer, nearly running as she reached the stairs. She didn't look back. Two minutes went by before he turned and walked away.

Life in Boston

Colin hadn't seen Mary in five weeks. He went to her employer's home three times and left notes but was always told she wasn't available.

He began spending late afternoons watching the symphony practice. Colin met the conductor and learned he was indeed from London, knew of St. Anne's and its choir, and had attended Oxford with Choirmaster Thomas. He let Colin play the piano when rehearsals were done and was impressed by the young man's natural abilities with the instrument.

His father embraced Mary's absence in a manner far too smug for his son. Warren arranged dinners for Colin to meet more acceptable young women.

The first was Priscilla Whitney, the daughter of a prominent businessman whose company supplied Phelps Industry with metal goods and provided an occasional contract for shipping parts. Priscilla was accompanied by her mother, an overly prim woman with an obsession for the latest fashion, and a keen interest in seeing who else was in the restaurant and whether they were noticing her. The younger Miss Whitney seemed endlessly impressed with herself and prattled on and on about her plans to spend the summer touring Europe. Rome, she felt, would suit her nicely, if the sun wasn't too much for her delicate skin. And the artwork in Paris might just inspire her own well-developed sense for combining charcoal with watercolors. "Aren't I a talent, Mother?"

"Of course, dear. And you'll bring back grand ideas for decorating the perfect home one day."

Colin wondered if she ever stopped talking.

The second candidate was Miss Catherine Blanchard, a nearly opposite experience. If Catherine had any grasp for the art of conversation, she was loath to show it. Warren would offer subjects and ask questions to draw her out, and she would answer with short, cursory words, blushing as if revealing deeply private personal information. Colin wondered if she'd ever been let outside her house.

She was attractive enough but too empty, too reticent to be good company. He hoped his father would end his campaign, but Warren seemed more determined than ever.

Saturdays were still devoted to *The Liberator*, helping Ben, and learning the printing process. He came to think of Ben as his closest friend. They discussed their prior lives. Ben was a fount of sage advice. The early cruelties of his life, the endurance it took to survive, and the gentle, quiet Quaker teachings had evolved in him a sense of patience, wisdom, and even optimism. His perspective now was that of a family man, a father who knew the joys of children and the security of a good woman's love.

Colin was invited to be their guest for a Sunday picnic on the banks of the Charles. He laughed as Ben pranced about with Noah on one shoulder and Sarah on the other. Ben twirled, making noises like a horse, then leapt with large strides as his children giggled.

Rebecca smiled, handing Colin an apple and gesturing toward Ben. "He'd play all day if he could. Never seen a man so full o' joy." Colin thought of the one picnic he could remember with his parents. These children were blessed; they would always have their family together.

Ben set the children down and took a large, colorful book out of their basket. He sat on the blanket while Noah leaned against him, his arm resting on his father's shoulder, looking down at the book. Sarah sat on his lap. Ben pointed to a picture of a duck. "Duck, D

U C K duck. What does a duck say?" Noah made a quacking sound. Ben nodded approval and pointed to a cow. The exercise continued for twelve animals. When the book was done, Ben took a stick and formed a fish in the dirt. He pointed to it and said, "Fish. What does a fish say?" Noah looked perplexed. Ben roared in laughter, tousled the boy's hair, and gave him a hug.

"He's set; these two 'll learn to read before they turn six. Loves the written word."

After they ate, Ben noticed Colin staring at a couple strolling arm-in-arm along the river. "Still think'n' o' her? She likes you, ya know."

"What makes you think she likes me?"

"She saw you three or four times, yes? Showed you how she danced, cared about your music. She's attracted to you. But she knows what's ahead. Irish are the bottom of the barrel, just above us Negroes. Cain't get work, folks think them dishonest, or worse. Knows your daddy wud blow dat candle out soon as it was lit. Both your hearts will be broken. She likes you well anuf. But cain't lose her job. That girl might be her family's sole support."

"She won't see me."

"How thick is your head?"

"What do you mean by that?"

"Showed you where she lives, how she lives. Girl did her part. Now 's all on you."

Colin sat up, his arms crossed in front of his chest. "You think my father will relent?"

"He loves you, don't he?"

The next evening, he went directly from the factory to the Worthington home, a clutch of flowers in his hand. Pacing outside the door, practicing what to say, he smoothed his hair back before knocking. The servant who answered was a severe-looking older woman, who spoke with a German accent.

"No. Mary not here. She loze ze pozition. Will not come back. Gute nacht."

Lost her position? A thought sprang into his head, a suspicion his father had intervened.

Ben Evicted

Ben finished running the first proof, preparing for his careful, painstaking check for errors, when a loud crash from the hallway caused him to stand. He turned halfway toward the door as three men burst in, two with pistols, one with a shotgun.

"Well, lookie here! Mister High-and-Mighty read'n' and print'n' up lies right here in the devil's workshop. Yer a long way from Virginia, nigger. But, hallelujah, we come to take you home. State your name, boy!"

Ben stood silent, judging his chances to escape. He might be able to take two of them, but not three, not with a shotgun present.

"Name, boy!"

"Johnson. Nathan Johnson. I'm a freeman of New York. You've no cause …"

"Ly'n' sack o' shit."

The butt of the shotgun was raised toward his face. Ben flashed to his mother's death. He lowered his shoulders and tackled the man, slamming him hard against the wall. The weapon fell to the floor. He grabbed the man's throat, squeezing with all his might before a pistol crushed the back of his skull. Ben collapsed, falling forward with his fingers still on his assailant's neck.

"I'll kill him! Filthy, God-damned nigger!" The man picked up the shotgun and pumped the stock. The other two reached out across his chest, blocking him.

"Hold! He's only worth half as much to us dead. You can watch him die back in Hopewell."

The man brushed them off. "He put his hands on me! He cain't do that and survive."

"Lester, if you shoot him, I swear, I'll cut your nuts off. Didn't come all this way for half our pay." He slowly reached out and guided the man's shotgun down toward the floor.

"You want some fun? … Destroy this place!"

That struck the right chord. Lester looked around as if in a brothel evaluating the talent. He smiled, then went to the large frame holding all the metal letters and yanked it over, sending thousands of pieces crashing across the floor. Then he picked up a heavy mallet and beat the press with strong smashing blows, mangling and distorting every part of it. He poured solvent onto the floor and was about to light it when they heard yelling outside. The guard they'd disabled had recovered. He was outside screaming for help.

"Come on, we gotta go!"

They lifted Ben under his armpits and supported him between them as they dragged him through the door. When they emerged, the guard stopped yelling, turned, and ran away. His commotion, however, attracted the attention of law enforcement. Two officers on horseback intercepted the men at the end of the block.

"You there! Stop and explain yourselves." One drew his nightstick from the saddle, knowing it would be of little use if his authoritative tone and uniform failed to hold sway.

"No need for concern, constables, we're here carrying out our lawful responsibilities under the Fugitive Slave Act. This man is the property of one Oliver Enders of Hopewell, Virginia. We have an affidavit from Mr. Enders, and his contract employing our services. You will, no doubt, be glad to see Boston free of another Negro."

The officers exchanged glances. They were no fan of the law, but the Fugitive Act required them to assist slave catchers or face considerable fines and prison themselves.

"We shall require your help in bringing him before a magistrate so that we may remove him from your city as expeditiously as possible."

A routine day at Phelps Industries was drawing to a close. Mr. Newton was returning by train from New York but had been delayed by a faulty locomotive. Colin was waiting to confront his father over Mary Dowling when Warren signaled for him.

"There's a delivery at the loading dock. Newton always checks them, but he's not back yet." He handed a bill of lading to his son. "Go check the supplies and see they're put up properly."

Colin stared at his father, wanting to ask him about Mary being sacked, but thought it better to wait until they were alone. He went to the dock, helping the driver unload boxes of heavy parts. The last one felt lighter than the others. That struck him as odd. He checked the bill, which called for twenty-four boxes. Only twenty-two were delivered, and the last box was only half full.

"You're missing two-and-a-half boxes. I can't sign for this."

The man looked flustered. "I'm sure it's right. Mr. Newton always supervises deliveries; he must have received the other boxes last month."

"We'll see about that when he's back. For now, I'm marking that you're short. We paid for more than we received." He was about to inspect the lightest box when he heard yelling from the front. His father was running toward him, beckoning other men to follow.

"They got Ben! Slave hunters. He's been captured!"

Colin joined his father and four of his employees as they streamed into the street, boarding wagons for the courthouse. When they arrived, the judge was just calling up the case. The bounty hunters approached the bench with Ben in chains, dried blood on the back of his head, swaying between them. Ten policemen were in the courtroom, anticipating trouble.

Warren shouted, "Your honor, this person is my employee. He is a free man with a wife and two children, earning gainful employment. There's no cause for this!"

The judge rapped his gavel several times. "There will be order. The bailiff will enforce silence during these proceedings. Do you men have an affidavit?"

"We do, your honor, sworn and attested to in the State of Virginia. We are in complete accordance with the Fugitive Slave Act and seek only your order that we may lawfully return this property to its rightful owner."

The judge motioned for them to approach and asked to see their paperwork, putting on spectacles to review the documents. After reading them, he looked at Ben. "Your name Benedictus Smith?"

Ben looked at his shoes.

Colin came forward. "Please, Judge, I can testify on his behalf."

The judge peered at him above his glasses. "There are no witnesses allowed, no testimony in a Fugitive case. It's federal law, and I'm obligated to grant these men their request, or I, myself, will be in legal jeopardy." He signed the form, followed by two more raps of the gavel. "Petition granted. The property is to be restored to its rightful owner. The bailiff and members of the Boston Police Department will escort these gentlemen safely to the train station."

Colin rushed toward Ben but was blocked by two officers. "Please don't take him. I'll buy him, please? I'll pay!"

No one acknowledged his pleas as Ben was escorted away.

Warren pulled his son to him in a large embrace, steadying him. "Now you know, son. Now you know."

Banking on a Loan

Colin sank onto the bench, breathing hard, trying to think of anything they could do. And then something else occurred to him. He looked up at his father, "We need to get to *The Liberator*."

When they arrived, the guard was standing staring at the mangled press; the letters strewn across the floor and papers soaking in solvent. He was startled when Colin and Warren walked in, then backed away so they could inspect the damage.

"Dear, Lord," he said, shaking his head. "What have they done?"

"They want us destroyed. The judge never knew about this. It's criminal destruction of property. We've got to bring them back, make them pay. Colin, get to the depot, see if you can find them. I'm going for the police."

He gave a look to the guard that said, "why didn't you stop them?" The guard gave a dejected shrug.

The southbound train was still in the station, but the slavers were nowhere to be found. Their plan had always been to leave by ship, with passage booked in advance. Any rabid abolitionists seeking revenge or trying to stop them at the train depot would be disappointed. They beamed with satisfaction, raising more than one glass of bourbon, toasting the destruction of *The Liberator*. It was an unexpected bonus. They would be celebrated as heroes throughout the South.

William Lloyd Garrison surveyed the damage done to his cherished press, his voice of reason to the world. "What wonton destruction! I've known evil my whole life, but I still wasn't prepared for this."

Warren put a hand on Garrison's shoulder. "We'll go after them, and we'll rebuild. Our next edition will tell the world what they've done. Let the nation know the kind of man Ben is. We'll rouse an army to his rescue."

Garrison was silent for a long time, then, in nearly a whisper, "We'll not give them the satisfaction. We will publish as usual, as if nothing happened. Nothing affected us at all."

"How can we?"

"I've friends at the *Tribune*. We'll contract with them to print our next few runs, until we procure another press and get back on our feet. No one will still our voices, not even for a day."

The *Tribune* agreed to print *The Liberator* for three weeks, but only after Warren pledged to pay for additional guards around the clock. In the meantime, he would arrange a loan from his bank to cover the unexpected costs. Normally, he would have sufficient reserves on hand, but a large order for railway casings had required him to layout a considerable amount for supplies.

The bank was happy to meet with him. Warren's business was a good depositor but, until now, had never required their lending services.

"Certainly, Mr. Phelps. Of course, Mr. Phelps. We will be delighted to assist you. A quick evaluation of the company's books should allow us to finalize the loan by the end of the week." Warren asked his son to deliver the books that afternoon.

Joseph Newton still hadn't returned from New York. Colin knew where he kept the ledgers and collected them from his office. It was crucial to get the bank's swift approval for *The Liberator* to continue without interruption. He tucked the books under his arm and sprinted the length of the factory floor, jumping onto his father's wagon and lashing the reins at the horse. The bank would have their records before close of business.

Joseph Newton's brother met him at the station when he arrived in Boston. Joseph smiled contentedly when Thaddeus told him about Ben and the newspaper. Warren and his boy would be too preoccupied with the paper to pay much attention to the business now. He would have a free rein.

Two days later, Warren strode confidently across the bank's lobby. He had calculated the amount needed to satisfy *The Tribune* and keep their weekly edition printing without interruption. The figures were set out on the paper rolled up in his hand. He raised that arm, signaling the bank president and flashing a broad smile. Mr. Randall smiled back weakly, almost avoiding Warren's eyes.

"I've all the numbers," Warren said. "They're higher than we discussed, but I wanted to include some contingencies in the loan."

The bank president ushered him into his office as if sneaking a mischievous dog into his room. He motioned toward a chair and circled to his side of the desk, sitting without looking at Warren, taking a deep breath, then opened two ledgers where they were bookmarked and, turning them around, slid each across the desk.

"Perhaps you've an answer for this."

Warren sat straight up with a questioning look. Mr. Randall stretched out his hand, resting his index finger on the first book. Warren bent over it.

"Two ledgers. One contradicts the other. Which am I to believe? This one seems to show a prosperous enterprise, while this one shows you losing money at an alarming rate."

Lazarus of Georgia, 1858

A young slave lay curled in the fetal position on a thin layer of damp straw. He dreamt he was on a raft floating to freedom, could almost see the shore, when a sharp pain struck his ribs, forcing him to wince and curl onto his other side.

"Get up, you filthy black bastard! You've got one chance to save your worthless life, and I'm it!"

The boy opened his eyes to a pair of muddy black boots pressed up close to his face. Looking up, adjusting to the darkness, he saw a large, bearded white man with sleeves rolled up and a bullwhip curled in his hand. The halo of light from a kerosene lantern was just enough to let him know he was in an animal's stall.

"Master may a' won you in a card game, but you ain't so cheap. He's gonna have to feed you now and clothe you at some point. You gots to earn it. You're gonna git up with the sun, and be ready to work, or I'll break both your legs and feed your sorry bones to the pigs. They love feast'n' on black flesh."

The boy planted his hands on the floor, pushed his way into a near sitting position, then scrunched away and flattened his back to the wall of the barn. Pain erupted throughout his body. His mind flashed to the previous week. He'd been caught after his escape. The dogs found him hiding deep in a swamp, and he'd been hauled back to master Turnbull's plantation. His mother had screamed and begged for mercy. Turnbull laughed and ordered the boy tied to a tree, then beat him nearly to death while his mother raged and sobbed.

When he recovered, Turnbull changed the boy's name to Lazarus. "Should a' died. Ain't never seen a nigger take that kind a whoop'n' and survive. He cain't escape my farm no more, but that boy sure did escape death, at least this time."

That night, he wagered the boy and his mother in a card game and lost them both. "Good riddance. They's noth'n' but worthless trouble."

Winslow Price owned them now. Three kings and a pair of nines had won the hand, and he had them loaded onto his wagon. The mother proved to be of little value to Price. He wondered if her son would be as worthless as she.

Pain flashed through the boy's body. The burly man pushed his boot against the slave's stomach, adding more pressure as the boy flinched. "They say you's named Lazarus now. That's a powerful 'nuf biblical name. Well, we got someone else here from the Bible, too."

He turned and yelled, "Bring him!"

A thin man with stooped shoulders approached, dragged really, by a large muscular German Shepherd with long, matted black fur. The dog strained at his leash, hurrying to the stall where the slave lay. His handler loosened the leash just enough for the beast to lunge at the boy without quite reaching him. The animal's nose curled back, exposing his full set of sharp teeth. Drool dripped from the corners of his mouth, while his slow, sustained growl filled the air.

"Here's a kick," the man laughed. "You know what this beast is named? It's Satan! He's gonna guard you tonight. Ain't that right, Satan? You won't let him go, will ya boy?" He flashed his whip, striking the floor inches from the dog. Satan yelped, quickly backed away, and cowered, but was snapped into place by the man holding his leash.

"Now listen up, boy! Satan will sit right here all night. If you try to leave this stall, even for a minute, you'll have a new name. They'll be calling you Scraps." He chuckled, instructing the animal to "Sit!" then removed his leash. "Stay!"

Lazarus still felt the pain of every blow he'd taken. The welts on his back where he'd been lashed, the scrapes on this knees and elbows where he been dragged to the tree, and the fists that landed on his jaw and ribs all felt fresh. He was in too much pain, and too exhausted, to care what the dog might do. He rolled slowly over on the straw with his back to the animal and fell asleep.

Soon, the slave was whimpering and shaking in his sleep. His whining sounded like a mixture of soft yelping and high-pitched crying. Satan was lying down, his head on his paws, listening to the sounds. He opened his eyes, raised his forehead, crawled closer to the boy, then sat up and cocked his head, watching Lazarus's heavy breathing.

The dog moved closer, licking the boy's swollen red elbow. Lazarus moaned. Satan pushed his snout under the boy's arm, putting his nose onto the slave's chest. The boy turned over, wrapping his other arm around the dog as Satan lay beside him. Together, they snuggled through the night.

Through all his pain, the closeness of the dog provided more comfort than Lazarus had experienced in years. He woke just before daybreak and began stroking Satan behind his ears. He felt the dog's heavy breathing beside him, thinking, *This ain't a beast. He's a slave too, like me.*

Mr. Price

A rooster crowed as the barn door slid open. Satan sat up, quickly resuming his guard position. Lazarus held his breath, expecting the worst. He opened his eyes, looking for last night's tormenter.

Instead, an older African woman approached, carrying a bucket of water, a handful of rags, and a small satchel. Satan lowered his head, growling as he padded in a semi-circle around her.

"Be still, dog! I don' means you no harm."

Satan knew her. He kept his eyes on the woman but let her pass.

"Well, you's alive. Dat's a thing, fo' sure. Thought I might find ya gone t' heaven by now. Let's take a look."

She put the bucket down next to him and knelt to examine the boy. Her head shook back and forth. "Em, mm, mm. No, sir, ain't no cause for dem to treat a soul dis way."

She drew a cup from inside the bucket and offered him a drink, which he took with trembling hands. When he was finished, the woman dipped a rag into the water and began carefully wiping the blood and dirt from his face.

"Why, you's noth'n' but a boy. Cain't be no mo' dan fifteen. An' almost gone to Jesus!" She squeezed the rag, letting water, blood, and dirt drain into the straw, then dipped it in the bucket again. "You let Constance take care o' ya. I'll get ya well, though dat might be a bigger curse. Work you t' death instead o' lett'n' ya die here in yer sleep."

Constance brought the rag up to his bruised ribcage. Lazarus flinched. She softened her touch. "I 'spect some o' dem's broken.

You cain't be no good fo' da field, not yet. If massa want you t' work at al', he best be lett'n' you rest." She washed his neck and chest, stopping to examine a star branded onto his shoulder.

"Someone dun branded you! Turnbull don't do dat. Who branded you?"

He shrugged weakly and just said, "Cuba, before we got stolen." Constance shook her head, making a disapproving, clucking sound.

She opened the satchel saying, "Two biscuits and a slice a ham is all we could spare. Might want t' save it. No tell'n' when you'll eat again." Having done what she could to clean and comfort him, Constance hurried out to attend her normal chores.

Lazarus sat on the floor with his back against the stall, his knees bent up in front of him. He pulled a biscuit out of the bag, taking a large bite and savoring the taste, unable to remember the last time he'd eaten. He polished it off, licked his fingers to get every crumb, and reached into the bag again. Lazarus brought out the last biscuit, spread it open, and placed the ham inside. Then he divided it, holding half of it out in the direction of the dog. "You be need'n' dis too, I 'spect."

Satan approached suspiciously. He sniffed the offering carefully, then swiftly chomped the food from the outstretched hand and devoured it. The dog softly padded closer, putting his head up against the boy's body. Lazarus stroked his fur. The slave closed his eyes, lowering his head onto his chest, and had fallen asleep when the sharp crack of a whip startled him.

"Git up, boy. Mr. Price wants to see what he won, see what you look like by daylight."

The man stood aside, revealing an immaculately dressed tall gentleman, perhaps in his mid-thirties, wearing a long, beige suit coat over a dark blue vest that covered a pleated white shirt. A wide bow tie rode under a winged collar, just below his well-trimmed beard. Creased slacks led down to highly polished, English riding boots. A broad-brimmed hat was held at his side. The man's sandy-brown hair was parted in the middle, flowing down near his shoulders. As he stepped toward the slave, his long shadow climbed the wall, expanding nearly to the top.

Mr. Price looked at the slave and winced. "You're worse than I expected, boy. Seems I may not have won my wager after all. What's your name?"

The boy tried to stand but slipped and collapsed onto the floor.

"You got a name, boy?"

"George, sir," he whispered.

"Mr. Turnbull said you cheated death, renamed you Lazarus. Judging from the look of you, that's a far more fitting name. I think we'll keep it. Can you stand?"

Lazarus reached up, clutching a rail and pulling himself to a standing position. He felt panicky and trembled. A wave of pain and nausea swept over him. He swayed, turned his head to the ceiling, and passed out, hitting the ground hard.

Price shook his head. "Turnbull should've paid me to take this rubbish off his hands. I'm late for church. See if he can be revived. We might still get some work out of him."

"Yes, sir."

"Give him a few days to recover. He's young enough, might last a few years if we get him restored. I expect he's lost his appetite for freedom."

For three years, Lazarus George, as he came to be known, bore every hardship Mr. Price and his hands imposed on him. After his recovery, he was made to clean stables before breakfast, work in the fields until after sunset, and clean farm equipment before being allowed his meager supper. But they could never frighten him with Satan again. The dog sought him out, wagging his tail when the overseer tried to set the dog against him. The slave always saved a secret morsel of food for Satan. Every week, Lazarus George watched and planned his escape. He always knew Satan would come with him when the time came.

ACCOUNTING

WARREN climbed the brick steps to his front porch, stopping just outside the door, his hand cradling the knob, his shoulders slumped, shaking his head. With a deep breath, and slight shudder, he inserted his key.

He sank into his wingback chair, refusing to look at the business ledgers on his lap. How could he have been so stupid, so negligent? Obviously, Newton had taken constant advantage of him. But if it was so obvious, how could he have missed it? He reviewed every image of the man. It was Newton who introduced him to the business, negotiated the terms of its purchase, always seeming to have Warren's best interests at heart. His whole demeanor had been that of an obsequious and respectful servant.

Then he recalled how eagerly Newton encouraged Warren to take all the time he needed away from the factory, how he praised his work at *The Liberator* and assured him all would be well at the plant. Warren realized the business he intended to leave to his son might soon be lost. He hurled the ledgers across the floor.

Colin was eager to get home, almost bouncing as he walked. He'd been developing a plan to rescue Ben, saving his money. He decided to go to Virginia with two of the biggest men from the factory and offer to buy Ben's freedom. If the owner refused, they would sneak onto the farm at night and spirit him away, using force if necessary. It would take a significant sum to finance the rescue, but his father would surely agree to it, and other abolitionists would help with finances.

He came home to discover Warren slumped in his chair, his legs stretched out in front of him, his head in his hand. He saw the journals halfway across the floor.

"What's happened, Father?'

Warren turned his head, slowly eyed his son, then stared at his shoes.

"There won't be any loan. We may lose the business."

"I don't understand. How could ...?"

"Newton's been stealing from us. He's been sly enough to siphon off revenue steadily, covering it with false receipts and fraudulent accounting entries. Our bank balance is nearly negative, and they've no interest in lending us even one dollar. I fear *The Liberator* is lost as well."

"But how ...?"

Warren pointed to the journals on the floor. "The ledgers don't agree. They're false. See for yourself."

Colin picked them up, keeping a questioning gaze on his father as he moved to the dining room table. He put the journals side by side, not sure what to look for. Numbers and math always came easy to him, but he had no training in accounting, knew no easy way to understand what the ledgers were telling him. Patiently, page by page, he studied the rows and columns, the descriptions of each entry, its purpose and cost. He was beginning to comprehend the implications when he turned one more page. Scrawled at the bottom of the page were the words: HOPEWELL, VIRGINIA, OLIVER ENDERS.

He grabbed the book, took it to his father, and held it out to him. "This is how they found Ben! Newton must've sent word to Virginia. The bastard likely received a reward." He wanted to say, *and you hired him,* but didn't.

He was breathing heavily, fuming. Ben was captured, Mary was gone, the factory and *The Liberator* might be lost forever. His father allowed all that happen. He shoved the book into Warren's hands and stormed out.

His father watched him go, unable to move for several minutes. His jaw and fists clenched tight as he went to the fireplace and grabbed the long metal poker. He might lose everything, but Joseph Newton would never spend another day upon this earth. He burst from the house, staring straight ahead, his legs taking forceful strides, the poker swinging by his side, his angry manner warning pedestrians out of his way.

Colin was already at the factory. Newton wasn't there. Warren insisted on searching anyway, stalking the floor, the poker held high, exploring every potential hiding place. His son followed quickly behind him, urging reason. "Killing him won't solve anything. Put that down. We've ample evidence to have him arrested. Let him rot in jail; we've got to save the business."

Warren ran out of steam. He sat on a large crate, dropped the poker onto the concrete floor, and fixed his eyes on the ceiling. "When I see him, I will kill him."

"No, you won't. If you do that, I'll lose you, too. I won't see you hanged over the likes of Joseph Newton. We'll get through this. Tell me what to do."

His father looked at Colin for a long time, as if he'd forgotten where they were. He slid down from the crate, picked up the poker, turned to survey every area of the factory, and said, "I've been through worse. I built this for you, and I'll be damned if I let anyone take it from you. Stay here in case he returns. I'll get the police."

Colin nodded, then headed back to Newton's office. He opened each desk drawer, looking for evidence. The sight of a crystal inkwell next to a gold letter opener angered him. There were folders of contracts in a file cabinet behind the desk. Colin wanted them preserved. He found two keys in the middle draw of the desk and locked everything. A thin metal spike on the edge of the desk held receipts and notes pierced onto it. Colin studied them but couldn't find anything incriminating. He paced and waited.

Warren returned with a couple of uniformed patrolmen and an older gentleman he introduced as Detective Hudgins. While they discussed what they'd learned and the gravity of his crimes, Newton rounded the corner from the loading dock. He pulled up sharply at the sight of so many people in his office. He gave one last look, a quick turn, and he was gone.

Detectives eventually discovered which bank account he'd used, and also that it was emptied the day his crimes came to light.

Father and son spent weeks questioning workers, suppliers, deliverymen, and anyone who might know about his practices and, most especially, his whereabouts.

The bank understood Warren had been victimized and offered to work with him. It recommended an accountant, who took control of the books and began amending contracts to eliminate waste.

Salvaging *The Liberator* was a more delicate matter. Without admitting the possibility of financial ruin, Warren was able to persuade wealthy friends to cover the costs at the *Tribune* and the purchase of a new press.

Ben's Fate

For several months, father and son worked from before sunrise until long after sundown. New orders were pursued, cost efficiencies were put into place, and workers were asked to do more for less. It was a slow, painful process, but it bore fruit.

Colin hadn't forgotten about Ben. He continued to save and planned to petition some of *The Liberator*'s patrons for contributions to buy freedom for his friend. He approached Abbey Kelley, who made a generous gift and offered to introduce him to other sympathetic donors. The promising start soon met with a hopeless end. It was halted at his next request.

Joshua Stevens, the next donor he approached, had business interests in Virginia. Mr. Stevens had heard the news, and it was confirmed. Slavers, newly arrived from Boston, celebrated as heroes, had ridden proudly on horseback as they paraded Ben through the streets of Hopewell, naked, with his hands bound behind him. A boy on a pony preceded him blowing a bugle. Townspeople gathered to enjoy the spectacle and hurl fruit or stones at the slave. He was ceremoniously presented to his master, Mr. Oliver Enders, in the town square. All the slaves from his farm were forced to attend.

The head of the militia read the order from Boston's court affirming the Fugitive Slave Act, and a second proclamation from the militia declaring that spoiled property should be disposed of when no longer useful. A large metal barrel of tar was heating over an open fire. Ben was dragged to the barrel where a militiaman ladled hot oil over him, front and back, taunting him for screaming.

Instead of feathers, copies of *The Liberator* were wrapped around his body. Benedictus Smith was dragged to an oak tree, hanged, and left to swing for three days, a lesson for anyone harboring hopes for freedom.

Colin raged at the news. He felt sick and had to be helped to a chair. He spent nearly a week in bed, curled in the fetal position, unable to eat. Colin might have continued that way but for a thought that occurred to him. Did Ben's wife know? He remembered their picnic together, Rebecca with little Noah and Sarah. Did they know? Would he have to tell them?

She had just finished the wash and was hanging children's clothes out to dry when Colin approached. Rebecca dried her hands and held them out to him weakly. "What news have you brought? Is there information from Virginia?"

His head fell, his chin nearly touching his chest. "It's too late." His moist eyes rose to meet hers. "I'm so sorry. Even if we'd been there the first week, we'd have been too late."

Rebecca held her hand out, resting it on Colin's cheek. She whispered, "I knew that. I never thought we'd see him again. Please, come inside. The children will be happy to see you."

Colin felt awkward, ashamed, following her into her home. Sarah looked as if she'd just woken from a nap, and Noah was on the floor guiding a small wooden horse through an imaginary kingdom. Both children brightened at seeing Colin. Their innocence touched his heart.

From then on, he spent nearly every Sunday afternoon, fulfilling Ben's hope for them, teaching Sarah and Noah to read.

The Last Straw

For the second Sunday in a row, Colin stood outside Mary's church. He watched everyone who came and left. She wasn't there. Her brothers weren't there. When the last person was gone, he checked his pocket watch. She could be on her way to the dance contest. He headed toward the Angel's Harp with brisk wide strides, covering the distance as if he was still keeping up with her.

He moved quickly from the front to the back room. It was dark and empty. Returning to the bar, he asked about the dancers.

"Season's over, lad. Won't begin again for six months."

"And what of Mary Dowling? Has she been in, or her brothers?"

"Not likely, heard they moved away."

"Moved where?"

The bartender shrugged as he wiped a rag across the bar. "Still serv'n' pints, so ya won't have wasted a trip."

Colin ordered a beer and drank slowly, looking for familiar patrons, anyone who might know her. Three hours later, he gave up. A few knew Mary, remembered her well, but did not know where she and her family might be.

He began spending weekday evenings and Saturday mornings working at *The Liberator*, helping where he could and reading past editions, missing Ben. He understood now why Garrison thought northern states should secede, why he felt a Constitution enshrining slavery was dishonorable, an affront to God.

Most Americans viewed their Constitution as a noble compact, but Garrison strongly disagreed. His first edition had declared:

"No body of men ever had the right to guarantee the holding of human beings in bondage. By the infamous bargain which they made between themselves, they virtually dethroned the Most-High God, and trampled beneath their feet their own solemn and heaven-attested Declaration, that all men are created equal."

Colin grew more and more an advocate for disunion.

He often thought of returning to England. If he didn't have to spend all his energy salvaging the business with his father, he would have relished sailing back to London. He wrote to Father McCall and his friend Malcolm. Their letters of reply were treasured, but news of life in England only fueled his urge to return. He kept their letters in a drawer of his desk in Newton's old office and read them whenever he needed a break. His latest letter to the priest declared, "This country is not the bright shining place I'd envisioned. There is much I can't understand. People in the South treat Negroes with inhuman cruelty while most northerners seem not to care. Abolitionists are treated as oddities. My father's business has been robbed and brought to the brink of failure.

"You'll be pleased to know I've taken to praying again. I ask for your prayers as well. I fear the strain on my father is more than he can bear."

The priest's next letter arrived four weeks later. Three paragraphs related stories of life at St. Anne's and updates on the boys Colin had been closest to. The fourth paragraph stunned him, scorching his last nerve:

Your father's promise over those first years meant a great deal to us. His charity allowed more students to attend our school. It enabled us to improve our library and chapel. While we were saddened he chose not to support us last year, please give him our heart-felt appreciation. We have been able to make do. I understand his means may not permit a gift this year as well.

Colin's jaw went tight; clenching his hands into tight fists, he pushed back from his desk and strode rapidly to his father's office.

One thing his father had promised was that St. Anne's could always count on his support.

Warren was inspecting a shipping list when Colin burst in. His son stood over him, breathing too hard to speak. Colin shoved the letter at him with a quivering hand.

"What's this, then?"

"Read it! It's from Father McCall."

Warren took it, putting on his glasses and bringing it closer to the light. He stood and moved toward Colin. His son moved away. "I had no idea. Newton was supposed to send the money the first of every year."

"And, again, you trusted him. St. Anne's counted on that money! You promised it would always continue through everything, good times and bad. As I recall, your finances were sound last year."

"Which I dearly meant. You don't think I would have condoned this if I'd known!"

"That's just it! You should have known!" Warren reached out to console Colin, but his son recoiled again. "You want to know what the last straw feels like? This is it!"

***

A strange thing happened in the fall of 1859. During the last two nights of August and first two nights of September, the largest solar flares ever recorded sent fear and wonder across much of the globe. The night sky was light as day. People woke at midnight and began making breakfast, thinking it was morning. Telegraph poles sparked. Most operators couldn't send or receive messages; others received messages when disconnected from power. Even in southern states, an aurora borealis of brilliant lights flashed across the heavens, changing from one hue to another, yellow fading into blue and green, then rolling into a soft purple.

Colin walked out onto the street, his eyes fixed on the lightshow overhead. Neighbors were out in force, some giddy, others terrified.

Perhaps this is the end of the world; perhaps the Messiah is coming at last! A woman fell to her knees, praying, shaking with heavy tears.

By Sunday the lights had subsided, but the churches were full. Abolitionists proclaimed the event was a final warning, a call to action.

John Brown, a radical Christian and fervent abolitionist, believed he was personally called by God to end slavery. He viewed the solar flares as God's vivid call to action. In just over a month, he raided the federal arsenal at Harper's Ferry. With the aid of two sons, fourteen whites, and five black men, he planned to seize its weapons and proceed south, arming slaves and leading a full insurrection.

The raid was put down in two days by Marines commanded by Lieutenant Colonel Robert E. Lee. Most northerners thought Brown was foolish, probably insane, but the incident sent shock waves throughout the south. Militias were expanded and re-armed in fear of a Negro insurrection. The Governor of Virginia elevated Brown to satanic status, urging the Commonwealth to secede. Most southern states were already planning to leave the union if a Republican won the presidency. The news of a white northerner seizing arms, intent on sparking a slave revolt, sent strong tremors throughout the south.

Downward

Colin's world closed in on him. Mary was gone. The promise to Father McCall had been broken. Colin clearly recalled the dinner at Rules Restaurant where his father had pledged constant support to St. Anne's.

Now their business was imperiled, and nothing would bring Ben back. Teaching Ben's children made him feel like an imposter. Making up for the loss of their father, when he, or his own father, should have known this could happen, should have protected Ben.

He confronted his father twice about Mary, and twice his father denied any involvement in her losing her job. "I couldn't even tell you her name, why would I care where she works? I'm sorry, but we've far more important matters demanding our attention."

By November, he took to sitting most nights at the Angel's Harp, downing pints, hoping she'd come in. At first, he offered money for information about her. Some took his dollars, but none really knew where she'd gone. He gave that up, and just drank.

Mornings were hard. His head throbbed, and his muscles felt weak. He did what he could for the business, but resented everything, his father most of all.

His father had let it all fall apart. Colin was convinced Mary's disappearance was also his father's doing somehow. Ben would still be alive if he'd been guarded more closely. They all knew he was a slave. They should have protected him. And Newton, robbing the business blind. How could that have gone unnoticed?

He liked the way beer and whisky made him feel. It numbed his frustration, took him outside himself. It also made him surly. He got loud some nights, protesting a world of "pompous frauds," demanding they admit their faults.

One night, he rocked back on his bar stool muttering slurred anguish to no one in particular, "You hate Negroes, you hate the Irish, you steal from one another." His head rolled sideways, and he stared blearily at the man next to him, a large fireman who wanted nothing more than to be left alone. "You're just as bad as the rest of them." He thrust out his arm, pushing the fireman off his stool. "You high and mighty blighters don't give a damn about anyone."

His tangled words slurred. He said, "Not one of you …" when the man rose from the floor, landing two swift punches to Colin's face, sending him over backwards. His head hit the floor with a loud crack, and his world went dark.

The bartender and fireman carried Colin out to the alley, rolling him away from the back door. The barkeep bent down, retrieving Colin's wallet, and taking out his money. "Ya don't want ta forget paying yer bill, d' ya?"

Assuming he survived, he was officially banned from the Angel's Harp.

Colin lay motionless for a long time. Cold mist fell over Boston, turning to sleet. He woke to a wet and frigid chill, thinking he was back on the streets of London. The world was out of sync. He turned over, placing his hands on the brick wall, using it to stagger upright. Keeping one hand on the wall, he took tentative steps toward the street, unsteady, as if the sea sickness from his voyage had returned. Blood pooled under his nose and ran down his chin. He rubbed it away with his sleeve and shivered violently.

At the street, he clung to a lamppost, trying to collect his thoughts, not understanding where he was or how he got there. His teeth chattered. He wrapped his arms around himself, but they provided no relief. Colin watched a wagon passing slowly by. He stared at it, trying to remember what it was. He squinted as the wagon went in and out of focus. His thoughts slowed, swirling and changing like porridge being stirred.

He stepped onto the street and was nearly struck by a two-horse carriage emerging from the dark, icy mist. The horses bucked, missing him by inches. Their driver cursed him and slapped the reins. Colin collapsed on the cobblestones.

A man in front of the Angel's Harp witnessed the near collision. He hurried to Colin's side and helped him off the street. "Ya were nearly killed. Are ya daft? And you're freezing!" He took his coat off and wrapped it around Colin's shoulders, guiding him into the pub.

He sat Colin next to the fireplace. The bartender saw them enter and started yelling, "That drunk's no longer welcome here. Put him back on the street!"

"Seamus, if I find you've played a part in these wounds, you'll be look'n' fer a new job."

"He's a rummy, spends all his time insult'n' patrons and asking fer Mary Dowling. If he was thrown out, 't was his own do'n'."

Colin slumped over the table, his head on his arms, moaning.

His savior stared at him, a light of recognition in his eyes. "You're Michael Dowling's friend." He nudged Colin. "Are ya the English lad? Do you know Michael and Brendan Dowling?" Colin's head barely moved.

"Well, we've met. I'm Tom Casey. I believe you helped me find a jacket. D' ya know where ya live?"

He moaned but didn't move.

Tom shook his head. "Fine. Let's get you warm; you can spend the night at my place. We'll find your home in the morning."

Colin woke in an unfamiliar room on a cramped sofa. Slivers of sunlight stretched across the floor. A wood-burning stove was dying, offering flickering gasps of flame. His head throbbed as he shivered under a heavy blanket. He stared at the ceiling, trying to focus, lacking the energy to turn and study the rest of his surroundings. His eyes fell shut, and he slept several more hours without dreaming.

The creaking of an opening door, and an icy breeze, woke him. The room was fully dark and cold. A match was struck, a candle lit, casting shadows across the ceiling. A silhouette moved to the stove adding wood, igniting it.

"Have ya slept the whole day, then?"

Colin turned to look up. "You brought me here, where am … Do I know you?"

"Thomas Casey. You and the Dowling boys helped me shop fer a coat."

"Oh yeah. I remember, slowly sitting up. "You know Mary?"

"Course I do, and I hear ya've been pine'n' away for her."

"Then you know where she is?"

"Moved. The whole family's in Milton now. Michael and the boys are stone masons at the church there."

"Milton. Where's that?"

"Not far. Ten to twelve miles south."

Colin sat up further, leaned toward Tom. "Is it because Mary lost her job?"

"Aye, it is."

He felt a tightening in his stomach, a dryness in his mouth. "Do they know who caused her to be sacked?"

"The whole family knows. Michael confronted him, pounding on the door, threatening him within an inch of his life. When the coward wouldn't come out, Michael threw a brick through his front window, the stained glass one. Likely irreplaceable. Screamed that Mary was owed wages, demanded that he come out."

"Stained glass? Whose house?"

"Worthington's, o' course. The bastard that attacked her."

"Wait, what happened?"

"The high and mighty lord o' the mansion took to follow'n' Mary around, touching her shoulder, sniffing her hair, running his hand down her back.

"The nights his wife went to suffragette meetings were the worst. He'd drink and follow her around like a wolf after a lamb. That night, he cornered her in the livin' room, grabbed her, and forced a whisky kiss on her. She slapped him, but he threw her onto the sofa. That's when Mrs. Worthington arrived, shriek'n' and stomp'n' her foot. Tossed a Bible at them and ordered Mary out of the house.

"Two nights later, Michael arrived with the brick. Worthington swore out a complaint, and the police had an arrest warrant issued. Michael's family needed to flee Boston for a bit. From what I hear, the Worthingtons are in Europe now, on the tour he'd always promised his wife, and she's show'n' off her luxurious new fur coat."

"I need to get home."

Reconciliation

Warren had been searching for his son since before dawn. He paced the parlor, cursing under his breath, angry that his son had taken to drink, frustrated by Colin's distance and his attitude of disdain. As the day wore on, he became more and more fearful of a tragic outcome. He knew he couldn't survive the loss of his son.

He heard footsteps on the porch and rushed to open the door. Colin, disheveled and aching, looked into his father's eyes. "I know you're mad …"

Warren reached out and hugged him for a long time. "Please don't do that again."

"I thought you had … I'm sorry. I was wrong. I won't give you any other cause for concern. I love you." He rested his head on his father's shoulder. Warren held his boy firmly, torn between exploding in anger and weeping in gratitude.

"If I'm to be any help to you in the morning, I'd best get some sleep."

"Stop! Listen for a change! I know you're disappointed in me. Working the business night and day isn't what you expected when I brought you to Boston. Well, life hasn't been easy for me either!

"Do you think I don't rue the day I left London, that I'm happy here? You've a right to blame me for a good many things. But you've no right to ruin your own life over it. You told me something in New York I can't forget, that thing Father McCall told you."

"And what was that?"

"He said every single second of life is carried with you into all eternity, that you remember every good thing, and every cruelty. It's a burden I carry. There are many things I hope to never think of again.

"Now I watch you, brooding, drinking, miserable in your own skin. If McCall is right, you're building a raft of terrible memories to carry with you forever."

Colin removed his hat, running his hand through his dirty hair, eyeing his father as if seeing him for the first time. He hadn't thought his father would have remembered that, and now he was struck to realize McCall's words might actually be true. He felt a chill.

Newsboys on the corner began shouting the evening headline: "Victory Declared! Lincoln Elected President."

Lincoln received no votes in ten of the fifteen southern states and won only two of 996 southern counties. The nation was more divided than ever. Boundaries were hardened.

MILTON

COLIN spent the rest of the week working harder and more diligently than he had in nearly a year. He was remorseful for the way he'd treated his father, ashamed of his drinking, and worried about memories he'd take into the next life, but mostly, he was excited and hopeful that he'd find Mary again.

He rose at five o'clock Sunday morning for a trip to Milton, confident he'd see her or her brothers at church. Snow had fallen overnight, and a steady wind pushed against him, blowing swirling white curtains across the road, slowing the horse, impeding his progress.

One gloved hand held a blanket tight around him, while the other held the reins. To pass the time, he sang Christmas carols from his days at St. Anne's. It steadied the horse and helped take his mind off the biting cold. After an hour, the sun peeked above the horizon, half hidden in clouds. He urged the horse faster, his own mind racing, planning what to say, imagining the outcome.

He arrived before the first Mass. Saint Agatha's was still under construction, with scaffolding running up the front and sides. But it was under roof and would offer warmth. He hurried inside, sitting in the back pew, watching the altar boys light candles and prepare for Mass. He shook the snow off his coat, rubbing his hands briskly to restore circulation. An organ rehearsed the morning's music. Colin looked at the stained-glass windows, arousing memories of St. Anne's. His emotions rose with the music; he prayed she would come soon.

The church was nearly full, with no Dowlings in attendance. Colin wished he'd paid more attention to Latin at St. Anne's. He craned his neck, watching everyone who entered. At Communion he studied each person filing toward the altar and back; he recognized none. Between services, he tended to his horse, and made inquiries to confirm this was the only Catholic church in town.

Parishioners were arriving for the second Mass, some in carriages, most walking. Colin climbed the steps and stood just beside the front door, searching every face. When he saw her, she was bundled in a large coat, a scarf covering half her face, one hand reaching up to her head to secure her veil against the wind. She was almost hidden in her wardrobe. But he would recognize her walk anywhere: the same energy, same graceful strides, Mary Dowling!

Her head was down as she started up the stone steps. "Mary."

She stopped, took a step backwards, looked up, holding his eyes in hers for a brief second. "So, you're change'n' yer religion now? We've Catholic churches in Boston, if ya recall."

Colin hadn't expected that from her; he struggled for a response. He couldn't take his eyes off her. "You're in this one. I hoped you'd give me another tour."

"Sure. There ya are again, think'n' I've noth'n better to do with m' time."

"I've missed you."

"A course ya have. Missed drink'n' w' me brothers too, no doubt."

"You didn't tell me you were moving. I've been looking for you."

"Lost me job."

"I could have helped."

"You'd have gotten me in more trouble. The likes o' you don't fit w' the likes o' me. I've been reminded of that more 'an once. Michael says it's time I understood that. Thinks I got in trouble by put'n' on airs. I'm a nanny now; me brothers have steady work. Life's simpler."

"Do you understand I care about you?"

"Me brothers warned me to avoid ya. I've had enough experience with high born. And here ya are, the Protestant son of an industrialist, standing outside a Catholic church in the snow. Can ya see how it does nae' fit?"

Colin looked down, his gaze resting on her shoes. He caught an image of her dancing.

"I don't have any music without you."

"Ya don't give up, do ya? Well, you can't walk me the whole way down the aisle, but I'll let ya take me halfway. It's freezing out here."

He held his arm out and escorted her inside.

She genuflected, tracing the sign of the cross before stepping into a row. Colin did the same. She knelt on the padded cushion, crossing herself again, closing her eyes to pray. He knelt beside Mary, keeping his eyes on her, wanting to put his arm around her, perhaps she'd lay her head on his shoulder, but didn't dare try. Having her so close sent a new energy pulsing through him. He wanted to protect her, cherish her, keep her near. He also wanted to know if she was even thinking about him at all.

A hymn was announced, and the congregation rose to sing "Adeste Fideles." It was one he'd performed often at St. Anne's. Colin joined in, perfectly voicing every note, carrying the feeling of the hymn with every verse.

It was Mary's turn to stare at Colin. She knew he played piano, remembered he'd been in a choir, but was captivated by his voice. When the song ended, she placed a hand on his arm and smiled appreciation. He covered her hand with his own.

After church, he asked to drive her home, suspecting she would decline. He didn't care about the condition of her home, only wanted to know where she lived. To his surprise, she agreed. A short ride took them to East Milton and a modest white house on a corner, 43 Emerson Road. It was a house far too small for the whole family, but a significant upgrade from her situation in Boston.

"Your brothers weren't at church."

"They've declared a builder's dispensation. Working the whole week at church lay'n' stone, entitles 'em a full day of rest on Sunday. Or so they've declared."

"A sound decision. May I walk you to your door?"

"May I remind you, we're not a good fit, and you've a long ride back to Boston."

"It's all a myth, isn't it?"

"What is?"

"America. The land of opportunity where anything's possible. Except it's not. Maybe if we'd met back home when I was a poor street urchin and you were a humble young lass from Tuam, Ireland, we'd have been made for each other. But forces conspire against us here. It's upside down."

"I've a family that needs support, and you've a father need'n' you in his business. Let's not tempt fate."

"I've never been more tempted in my life, Mary. I want to be reckless and joyful! I want to spend every day making you laugh, watching you dance, staring into those mischievous eyes of yours. I want my music back! I started a song for you, remember? And I want to finish it, no matter how many years it takes."

"Ya sure yer not Irish? You've all the blarney fer it, and a bit too much confidence. It's start'n' to snow again. Ya best be return'n' home now. Your Da will be worried. But, if I'm to be yer muse, I suppose ya could meet me Wednesday at four o'clock. It's me night off. Maybe you'll get another note or two."

Christmas Surprise

The next few weeks were all about Mary. Every Sunday and Wednesday evening, he spent as much time as possible with her. She kept guard of her emotions, but he could tell she was softening. More importantly, his father had softened. He no longer objected to "that Irish girl."

In fact, he suggested Colin invite her for supper on Christmas Eve. Although Christmas fell on a Tuesday and wasn't a national holiday, her employers gave her two days off to celebrate. She accepted his invitation.

He picked her up just before noon. It was a sparkling winter day under a bright blue sky, but the temperature was barely above ten degrees. They rode back under a large blanket, sitting close together for warmth. Gusts of white air streamed from the horse's nostrils, as it trotted back to Boston.

Colin noticed a large wagon pulling away from his home when they arrived. He jumped down and held a hand out, guiding Mary down, escorting her up the icy steps to the front door. They had just crossed the threshold when Warren greeted them warmly, giving Mary a respectful bow and saying, "Happy Christmas. Welcome to our home." She gave a slight courtesy and a nervous "honored to be here."

"Son, why don't you and Mary go into the parlor. She might like to hear you play a carol for the season."

Colin cocked his head sideways giving his father a questioning look.

"Go on. We'd all like to hear you play." He brought an arm up, urging them toward the next room.

They followed his request, and Colin stopped abruptly. A shiny, black, baby grand piano stood proudly by the bay window with a bright red ribbon atop, and a large card that read: "To Colin with love, Father."

"How …?"

"I've a few surprises left in me. And the business is doing well enough again."

Colin gave his father a quick embrace, then went to the bench, running his fingers reverently across the keyboard cover before lifting it and playing a chord. He grinned appreciatively, turning to Mary.

"You see, my music returns when I'm with you." She smiled, placing a hand on his shoulder. "Have you ever heard Bach's Christmas cantatas?"

"I don't know, but I'd surely love to hear them now."

An enjoyable afternoon of music, pleasant conversation, and laughter continued into the dining room. Warren's housekeeper had prepared a large meal of ham, mashed potatoes, creamed onions, hot rolls, and cranberry sauce. Warren poured wine and raised a glass in a toast to the season and to offer a formal welcome to Mary. Before he could bring it to his lips, a loud banging on the front door, and shouts from the porch, interrupted. He scowled, tuning his head to the hall, dropping a fist on the table and uttering, "Who in the world …?"

He went to the door, flinging it open intending to send the intruder away, but stopped short when he saw William Lloyd Garrison standing red-faced on his porch.

"It's happened! South Carolina has seceded! I'd say good riddance, but it means permanent enslavement if it can't be reversed."

Garrison nearly brushed Warren aside as he barged inside. "Here's their treacherous declaration. An allegiance to slavery above all else! Dated Christmas Eve! They've no fear of the Lord."

He shoved a newspaper forward. "Read it for yourself."

Northern States have denounced as sinful the institution of slavery; they have permitted open establishment of societies; whose avowed object is to disturb the peace and to eloign the property of the citizens of other States.

They have encouraged and assisted thousands of our slaves to leave their homes; and those who remain, have been incited by emissaries, books, and pictures to servile insurrection.

We abhor the election of a man to the high office of President of the United States; whose opinions and purposes are hostile to slavery.

He is to be entrusted with the administration of the common Government, because he has declared that "Government cannot endure permanently half slave, half free," and that the public mind must rest in the belief that slavery is in the course of ultimate extinction.

We, therefore, the People of South Carolina, by our delegates in Convention assembled, appealing to the Supreme Judge of the world for the rectitude of our intentions, have solemnly declared that the Union heretofore existing between this State and the other States of North America, is dissolved, and that the State of South Carolina has resumed her position among the nations of the world, as a separate and independent State; with full power to levy war, conclude peace, contract alliances, establish commerce, and to do all other acts and things which independent States may of right do.

Adopted December 24, 1860.

Warren handed the paper back to Garrison. "And I assume Buchanan has made no response?"

"May I remind you, our honorable president supported Dred Scott. He's without any backbone of his own, just counting the days until Lincoln takes the office from him. He'll not raise a hand or even a word against this."

Colin came in from the dining room. "Can they do that? Can a state simply absolve itself of any commitment to the nation as a whole? Won't Congress or the president block their exit? Why South Carolina?"

"Slaves are nearly 60 percent of the state's population. Owners would be terrified of letting them go free. You watch, other states'll follow, all to hold their Negroes under bondage."

"Lincoln won't be sworn in for three months. The government can't simply let half the nation slip away!"

But it *did* slip away, rather jubilantly. By February, seven states had seceded. A convention in Alabama declared creation of the Confederate States of America and elected the former Secretary of War, Jefferson Davis, as its president. President Buchanan refused to act, and Mr. Lincoln was completely silent, preferring to remain so until his inauguration on March 4th.

For northern businessmen it was a time of uncertainty. Previous lines of commerce were interrupted. Sources of goods from the south were drying up, and southern customers were disappearing.

A Call to Arms

Phelps Industries began to struggle again. However, Warren realized the North would need what his factory produced, more fabrication of rail and shipping goods, even armaments, if its economy was to survive. He made trips to Washington and New York, securing contracts that would grow significantly if all-out war should erupt.

Colin was busier than ever at the factory but still spent Sunday and Wednesday evenings with Mary. Her brothers teased him mercilessly, but with underlying fondness. They had to acknowledge he gave as well as he took.

All of them speculated about the prospect of armed conflict. Michael swore he hadn't come to America to fight its wars. Colin didn't relish the idea but thought about Benedictus Smith, his wife and children, about what the institution of slavery had done to them. The southern states had declared slavery to be permanently protected, with no peaceful means for change.

Mary said they should focus on what they could control and leave the rest to others. "Build the church," she instructed her brothers. "Mind yer father's business," she urged Colin. "I'll concentrate on caring for me employer's children, and we'll build our own lives. All else is folly."

For a time, that's what they did. But national tensions grew increasingly bitter every week. By Inauguration Day, mistrust and acrimony between the North and South had solidified.

Lincoln's address was meant to be an appeal for peace and reconciliation, "the better angels of our nature." But both sides were too entrenched to hear. He affirmed he had no intention of ending slavery: "I believe I have no lawful right to do so, and I have no inclination to do so."

He also had no intention to use arms unless necessary to "hold, occupy and possess the places and properties" of the federal government, but would use firm and appropriate force should the South take up arms against the government.

The new president was neutral on the expansion of slavery in the territories and promised to enforce the Fugitive Slave Act. The U.S. mail would continue throughout the South unless met with conflict, and he wouldn't use the spoils system to impose northern office holders on southern states.

Lincoln even expressed support for the Corwin Amendment to the Constitution, just passed by Congress. If adopted by three-fourths of the states, it would forever prevent Congress from limiting slavery: "No amendment shall be made to the Constitution which will authorize or give to Congress the power to abolish or interfere, within any state, with the domestic institutions there, including that of persons held to labor or service by the laws of said state."

For Warren and the abolitionists, the speech was total capitulation. The South treated it as a pack of lies. Nothing was resolved.

In just over a month, with threats to Fort Sumter in Charleston, Lincoln ordered the garrison to be re-supplied. The Confederacy responded by opening fire on the fort with fifty cannons. Over three thousand shells were hurled into its walls, forcing the Union to surrender. The war between the states had commenced.

Lincoln issued a call for the enlistment of 75,000 troops, and in short order, Virginia, North Carolina, Arkansas, Tennessee, and eventually Texas broke away.

Boston patriots were eager to heed the president's call. Parades, bands, and speeches swelled the hearts of young men eager to prove their bravery, excited by the adventure, confident in swiftly winning back the South.

Warren constantly reminded his son of his importance to the business. Colin could do far more to support the war effort by keeping the factory running at full speed. Mary was quick to echo his sentiment, and he accepted their advice.

Decision Made

In June, Colin asked Mary if she would forego church that week. There was someone he wanted her to meet. He hadn't attended church in nearly a year. Instead, before going to Mary's, he spent every Sunday afternoon at the home of Rebecca Smith. He would meet her and the children as they returned from their own service. Colin had rarely missed a chance to be with them and teach the children to read.

Mary knew the story of Ben, how he'd been captured, forced back south, and murdered in Virginia. Until now, it was more a story than reality. She brought a lemon cake and a scarf she had knitted and gave them to Rebecca when they were introduced. Colin gave a small bag of taffy to each child along with a batch of colored pencils.

He hugged the children and sat down with them on the floor. Colin took a large notebook from his briefcase and opened it for Noah and Sarah.

"Let's see. Where did we leave off?"

"The ocean," Noah said.

"Ah, yes. The ocean. Two baby bears had just set off to sea."

"In a sailboat filled with candy!"

"Yes. And do you remember the name of the boat?"

"It's Courage."

"That's right. Do you remember how to spell that?"

Noah proudly spelled the word. Mary noticed the book contained large, hand-drawn pictures, carefully colored in, with words below each one.

"And where is Courage going?"

"To save the princess," Sarah said.

"Yes. Who wants to decide where the princess lives?"

Sarah shot up her hand. "On an island."

"Perfect choice. Let's learn to spell island, it's a little tricky. Then you can draw it, Noah, and Sarah, you can draw the princess. What do you think she lives in on the island?"

"A palace!" Noah shouted.

"Of course. We'll learn to spell palace, too. You can show me how to draw it."

Mary had never seen Colin so animated, so engaged and alive. If anyone was meant to be with children, to teach and encourage them, it was Colin. She spent the afternoon talking with Rebecca, learning more of how she and Ben had come to Boston. She also noticed how well the children's clothes were made and discovered that Rebecca had made them herself.

"I've been sewing since I was a tiny girl. It's a skill my mother taught me, and one that's provided me a living."

"The family I work for is in need o' skills like yers. Can ya take on any more for a proper price?"

Rebecca looked at her children and sighed. "It would be a blessing to earn a bit more."

"I'll be see'n' to it, then."

Colin was silent the whole ride home, deep in thought. She touched his arm. "Why so quiet?"

"Slavery took their father, took her husband. Southerners could just reach up to Boston, grab Ben in their clutches, and do whatever they wanted to him."

"I know. It's horrible."

"Nothing's changed. This war's been waged for over a year; nothing's gotten any better. If anything, the rebels are winning. They're beating us on the battlefield and in the legislatures. Five northern states have already ratified the Corwin Amendment. I can't just sit in an office in my father's company and let it happen."

"Things'll change. It'll get better. You'll see."

"Really? How? It's going from bad to worse. You've met Rebecca, seen her children. What do you think's happening to Negro families in the Confederate states? Hell, they don't even keep families together."

Mary held his hand, reached her other arm up over his shoulders. She leaned toward him, focusing his eyes on hers. "God won't permit this to go on. Ya need ta place yer faith in the Lord."

"Have you not heard? God helps those who help themselves. It's tearing me up, Mary. Can you understand that?"

They were quiet for the final mile home. Mary gave him a tender kiss and begged softly, "Please don't do it."

It was too late. His mind was made up. Two weeks later he told his father he'd enlisted, insisting he was determined to do his part. He pleaded with Mary to understand, to wait for him, to pray for him. He promised that if he returned, they would never be apart again. Colin left three days later.

His letters were frequent. Army life was hard, messy, unkind, and lonely, but he had known worse as a boy, could tolerate it better than most, and would return to her.

***

September 16, 1862

My Dearest Mary, My Heart:

I trust these words find you well and enjoying the comforts of home. By now your dancing season is well advanced. I look forward to seeing your ribbons on my return. For my part, there is no comfort here but the memory of your blithe spirit.

We remain in the north. General Lee has pushed his troops into Maryland with the goal of converting her to the Confederacy. If that should occur, Washington will be surrounded. Virginia to the South and Maryland to the North. Lincoln will have no choice but to surrender. Some say he will be hanged, but I believe Mister Lee is too high a gentleman to permit such a disgraceful act.

Skirmishes have been frightful, but thankfully few so far. When the enemy is engaged, it's as if the gates of hell open up and shrieking demons chase after us. The stench on the battlefield is brimstone and blood. The deafening sound of thunder and the splatter of humanity assault from all sides. But I am resolute. My fight is in memory of Ben and all who remain enslaved.

Mary, I could never face this challenge without your love to brace me. Your memory lives with me everywhere. A patch of wildflowers reminds me of your laughter. The bright afternoon sun reminds me of your smile. When we are drenched with rain and my clothes cling tight around me, I'm reminded of your embrace. At night, the stars sparkle with the energy of your eyes.

I count the days, nay, the hours, and the minutes until I can be with you again. Please look after my father for me. Pray to God for my safe return, and victory for our cause. Yours in love, now and forever, Colin.

Last Battle

Morning fog rose across the field as the first shafts of light pierced the mist. Colin stared across the vast expanse with eyes that had known no sleep. A long line of Confederates was barely visible on the far ridge. Their cannons, however, could not be unseen, nor could the rebel officers on their horses trotting back and forth along the line, swords raised, encouraging their troops.

Birds were chirping. Colin realized these little feathered creatures might outlive most of those on the battlefield. Their tiny hearts would beat tomorrow, their songs unchanged.

His brigade was on the far-left side of the Union Army with orders to march against the end of the rebel line, outflank them, drive them in against themselves, and pinch them to the middle. If possible, they were to get behind the Confederate troops, sowing panic along a surrounded gray line.

Drums and bugles sounded the advance. Colin, in the third row of troops, marched in lockstep with his comrades, hearts nearly beating out of their chests, holding rifles with sweaty, quivering hands. They trudged through the high September grass, murmuring encouragement to each other.

A hundred yards into their advance, the Union cannons roared, sending balls high overhead, crashing into the Confederate defenses. A loud cheer erupted from the blue line. Soldiers picked up the pace. Nearly running, they brought their rifles up, firing volleys at the enemy. The rebel cannons had been silent until that point. Now they opened up, shredding men from the line, booming incessantly, terrorizing the troops.

The Union advance faltered. Two men fell dead in front of Colin. The sounds were overwhelming, horrible. Bullets and cannonballs turned the air into a terrifying metal storm. He knew escape was lost, forward or back; the air buzzed with death.

He tripped over a body. It was a man he knew well; he got to his knees, breathing uncontrollably, staring into the dead eyes of his friend. A bullet bit the grass next to him. He turned back to the battle and was about to rise when he heard a new sound erupting from behind him.

Union cavalry launched an attack on the middle of the Confederate lines. Soldiers on horseback surged forward, pistols and swords in hand, screaming curses at the enemy. With that, the rebels concentrated their fire toward the center of their lines.

Colin rose and helped rally others. It might only be a split second, but it was an opening. They began running full speed toward the far flank of the gray line. It was working! The enemy was focusing more attention on the cavalry charge, almost abandoning defense of their right side. Colin felt a spark of hope, an ability to breathe. The path to victory was clear. They would drive the enemy in on itself, fighting from behind them, avoiding front line fire.

Suddenly, a deafening howl resounded from the woods to their left, as if a thousand wolves had joined the fray. Rebel soldiers on foot and on horseback had hidden in the clump of trees, waiting for this moment. It was now the Union army that was outflanked. Colin turned to face them. He fired his rifle without aiming and had no confidence he'd hit anyone, nor that it would be much help if he did.

A bullet struck him in the left leg. He collapsed with the impact, dropping his rifle. Colin winced in pain, drawing his pistol, readying it to fire, turning to see a rebel nearly on top of him. He watched as if in slow motion while the Confederate raised his sword. He saw the glint of sunlight on the blade, watched it arc toward him, tried to block it with his arm, knowing it was too late. The enormous roar of the battle shrunk to the size of a thimble, and then there was silence. Nothing.

***

Warren Phelps followed the progress of the war in great detail. The South was winning at every turn. McClellan's Army of the Potomac had faltered under a commander too pompous and too cowardly to press the advantage. The siege of Richmond had failed, and Lee's army was now traipsing through Maryland. Morning newspapers carried discouraging news every day.

This morning was no different. Warren read the headlines. A battle fought to a draw last week had killed over twenty thousand on both sides, the bloodiest battle of the war. He quickly turned to the pages that listed "Union Dead," running his finger down the long column of names, and then he stopped short. His breath left him. He closed his eyes, rocked gently on his chair, and looked to read the name again. He sat completely still, slowly shaking his head.

Tears clouded his eyes. He staggered to the piano and rubbed his hand across the top, caressing it. His body shook as he sobbed uncontrollably. Then Warren banged the keyboard with both fists, harder and harder, before sinking onto the bench and sweeping the sheets of music off the instrument. He watched the pages flutter and fall to the floor, knowing the music had gone out of his life forever. He would have to tell Mary, but not today.

He looked at the pages and pages of names again. With so many dead, he realized they would likely be buried on the battlefield. Colin's body might never be returned. Warren would never know where his son was laid to rest.

Angel Insists

Two black men hurried through the battlefield in the dark, picking weapons and supplies from the dead on both sides. They alternated between gathering items and relaying them to a horse-drawn wagon at the edge of the field. A long-haired, black and tan German Shepherd ran ahead of them. It stopped in front of a body lying on its side, partially covering a rifle. The first Negro approached the body, reaching down to pet the dog with a "good boy." He rolled the soldier off the rifle and was reaching for it when the body twitched. A soft groan, more of a whimper.

"Dis un's alive."

"Leave him. Sun'll be up soon, and we got to be gone."

The man grabbed the rifle and swiftly pulled the pistol from the soldier's hand as he rose and headed toward their wagon. His quick strides covered thirty yards before he realized the dog wasn't following. He whistled, and shouted, "Come, boy." After another ten yards, he turned to see the dog sitting next to the soldier, a paw on the man's chest. "Come, damn you. We got no time to waste." The dog barked, raised his paw, and stroked the crumpled body. Another whimper.

"You fool dog! Dat un'll be dead a fore you ken scratch yer ear. Leave him!"

The animal refused to move. "Ah, fer Christ's sake, Angel!" He pulled on the dog's collar. "Come on now." Angel dug his paws into the ground, refusing to move.

"Joe! We need hep o'er here. Dog won't move."

"We got to skedaddle, George. Sojers be com'n' back any minute for their dead. Leave him!"

"You don't know Angel. Dis beast'll stay here till Kingdom Come if we don't hep dis soldier. Pick up his feet. I got his arms; les jus gets him to da wagon."

The dog followed at their heels while they loaded the soldier on the wagon with its cache of weapons and supplies. Angel hopped up and sat beside the dying man. "Damn fool dog." George snapped the reins, urging the horse forward.

By eight o'clock, they were well into the woods, following a path barely visible through high grass. Trees closed in around them, denser with every quarter mile. A shack at the end of the trail, nearly hidden in vines and foliage, had likely been a retreat for a hunter or trapper. A woman came through the door as they approached.

"Got ya some breakfast, if you's ready."

"We got somt'n' fer you, Constance, if ya got yer remedies. George's dog be want'n' to bring a man back from the dead."

She shook her head, looking down at the soldier in the wagon. "Wud you look at da gash on his head! An' his leg's all tore up. Lot a blood gone. I 'spect he's dead a'ready." Angel barked and seemed to smile. "Stupid mutt."

"Well, I saved you once, George, or shud I be say'n' Lazarus? But dis be a whole other sort. Sit'n' on the door a death. Be more merciful ta let him go."

"You tell dat to Angel, then."

"God a-mercy! Bring him inside."

She took great care cleaning the young soldier, applying herbal dressings and compresses on his wounds. She coaxed water down his throat, small drops at a time. The bullet had pierced his leg and gone straight through. Constance stitched the wounds as tight as she could, then prayed for his recovery.

Colin woke the following day, his head pounding, his mouth dry, and his leg throbbing. He was alone. He reached up, fingering a brass button on his uniform, turning to look at his surroundings. Nothing offered a clue as to where he was. He ran his hand gently down his leg, igniting pain and feeling the rough edges of stitches protruding front and back. Another mystery.

He started to yawn, but a tight cloth, likely taken from the battlefield, was wrapped tightly over the top of his head covering his left ear, circling under his chin, stretching up over the top twice and pinned near his right ear. His mouth could barely open. He groaned and tried to sound out "Hello." He tried again, louder.

This brought a response. Constance opened the door, holding a dead rabbit by its feet, a skinning knife in her right hand.

"Lordy, Lordy. You's a liv'n' breath'n' miracle a God." She put the rabbit down in front of the small fireplace and came to his side. He realized he was on an army cot. She brought a canteen to his mouth and let him drink his fill. Placing her hand on his forehead, she sighed, "Still too hot."

As he looked around, he saw one wall lined with rifles, pistols, swords, and bayonets. He brought her attention to them with his eyes. "George is arm'n' slaves. He and Joe been collect'n' weapons and sneak'n' em to the folks in da field. If da rebels win dis war, they gonna come home to a whole other battle on their hands." A weak smile. "Gonna pass dees ones out in a day or two."

Over the next five days, Constance nursed him as well as she could, humming gospel songs as she changed his bandages and applied her herbal wraps. She insisted he eat, fixing porridge for breakfast and an occasional stew when rabbits or squirrels could be trapped. He gradually gained strength and gathered the courage to ask if she had a mirror. He could feel where the sword had sliced his face from the top of his head, just missing the front of his left ear and down almost to his neck.

"Best I can do is the side of a pot. Besides, ya don' want to see that yet. It's close to yer hair line, likely a good deal will get covered o'er time. Let it be fer now."

"I have to see. Please."

She rubbed a pot with her apron and held it up for him to see. The image was smoky and distorted, but he could judge the size and shape of the gash. He fingered the rough stitches, and softly pushed on his swollen cheek. "Is it infected?"

"Treated it as best I could. Looks good fer now. Where ya from?"

"London."

"London, England? I done heard a lot, but you take da cake. Da British fight'n' for the Union now?"

"Sorry. Boston. Born in London, live in Boston now. I have to get home, have to let them know I'm alive."

"In time. You get well first. We can't give away our hide'n' spot or we all dead."

"For how long? I can't stay. Did we lose the battle? Is Maryland lost?"

She shrugged. "George said both sides lost. You git better, we'll git ya home."

"Is he your son?"

"George? No. Closest thing I got though. I nursed him back from death, same as you. Now he's repay'n' me. Tak'n' me north to be a free woman. 'Spect I'll be sixty in a year or two. He promised I'd be free by then."

"What about other family? Aren't they missing you?"

"Ain't got no family." She gazed at the row of rifles. "Had a daughter once. Elizabeth. Twer'n't really mine, I guess. The senior Mr. Price took me one night. Forced his self on me, and afore I know it, a baby's on da way. Dat l'l girl was the one bright shining spot in my life. She found joy in everything. Her laughter and her love was all I cared fer. She'd sleep up next to me at night and I'd feel her breath'n' like a tiny angel, all mine.

"Mrs. Price hated that child. I tried keep'n' Lizzy out a her sight 'cause it was no mystery a white man was involved. She called my daughter "that thing" and threatened to have her drowned. Seemed she'd forgot about her fer a time. Then, when Lizbeth was three years old, Mrs. Price gave her away. Gifted her to a cousin in South Carolina fer a wedd'n' present. I done never seen her again. That's when the light went outa my heart. Never will return.

"George promised, if ya win dis war, he'll take me ta find her. Can ya imagine? Me and my precious Lizbeth back together! You know I'm pray'n' like a fever for y'all ta win."

"I'll be praying you find your daughter again."

Burning Down the House

George and Joe returned the next day to collect their weapons. "You're look'n' better, sojer. Constance done worked her magic on ya. 'Spect we might get ya home afore too long."

Colin stood, clinging to the wooden cane Constance had fashioned for him. He limped forward, offering to help with the rifles.

"Don't be troubl'n' yerself."

"I want to help. Let me hand them to you, and you can hand them off to Joe."

When they were finished, Colin asked how long they'd be gone, and how soon before he could be on the move. They promised to be back in two days and, if his health permitted, they'd take him as close to the Union army as possible.

A heavy rain fell the second day, drenching the ground from morning until after sunset. Colin assumed it would delay their return, and he was right. It was 5 in the afternoon of the fourth day before George returned, with Angel at his side.

"How are things out there? Any news on the war?"

George laughed. "I been in Virginia, slipp'n' in mud, sneak'n' through back woods, hid'n' in barns, pass'n' weapons to slaves who could a turned me in any time. Got no news on yer war."

"And Joe?"

"He's scout'n' a next move."

"I'm feeling well enough to travel. You and Constance have been a Godsend to me. I hope to repay you generously one day, but I've got to get more medical attention, get home."

"It's Angel you shud thank. We was gonna leave ya in the da field."

"Well, I'm deeply grateful you didn't. How can I find you when this is over?"

"You just kill all the rebels you kin find. That be thanks enough."

Angel turned toward the door, letting out a low sustained growl. They heard horses approaching, followed by two gunshots. There was a moment of tense silence and then a loud shout: "We know you're in there! Come out peaceful-like, and we'll let you live."

George rushed to the back corner of the shack, beckoning Colin to follow. He lifted two wide floorboards, supported Colin by the shoulder to help him duck below, then urged Angel down and, followed him, returning the floorboards to their place. They were in an earthen cellar about five feet deep and six feet across running the length of the shack.

Another shout, "Last chance!" The door was kicked open, and shotgun blasts reverberated through the room. Heavy boots clomped across the floor. The sounds of furniture being thrown about were obvious.

George placed a hand on Angel's snout and gave a look that meant "silence!" The animal squirmed but remained quiet.

"Damn! Them boys is gone. Set this place on fire. Burn it to the ground! We'll find 'em yet."

"Wait! On second thought, if they see smoke, they'll hightail it outa here. You and Orville hide out in the woods behind this place. We'll try to catch them on the road, but if we miss 'em and they come back, you men'll take care of 'em. Let 'em get settled in, and when they're sound asleep, set this shack on fire and turn 'em into barbecue." They shared a hearty laugh. "Either way, we'll meet you back at Frederick Crossing in the morning. Oh, and drag that thing out back so they don't see it."

Colin and George listened as boots pounded back across the floor, and horses were ridden away. Their underground sanctuary was too small for the three of them. Colin's bent position was sharply painful.

Tears in his eyes, he tapped George and pointed up. George shook his head, holding up one finger: wait.

Five excruciating minutes passed before George slowly lifted the boards and raised his head. Angel jumped ahead of him, and George had to hiss, "Hold!" to keep the animal from running out the open door. He extended an arm to help Colin up. Colin stretched and rubbed his leg while George went to the fireplace and removed a few stones. He reached behind them and withdrew two pistols.

"Take dis un. We'll circle da house and get 'em in da woods. You go round dat way, I'll get 'em from dis side."

Colin pointed to his leg. "Remember, I'm slow. Wait for me to get into position."

They crept in opposite directions, George's left hand holding Angel's collar, a pistol in his right. At the back corner, they each peered around to see where the men were hiding.

Both saw her at the same time: Constance, lying face down in the mud with a gunshot to her lower back, and the top part of her head missing. Colin felt dizzy; he had to put a hand on the side of the cabin to steady himself.

George tried waiting to catch his breath, but Angel broke loose and bounded into the thicket. The dog raced full speed at one of the men, flying up, clenching the man's arm in his strong teeth.

The other man was sitting with his back to a tree. He jumped up, pulling a pistol and taking aim, not sure if he would hit the dog or his friend. Colin saw the man raise his weapon and fired his own pistol three times. Two of his shots found their mark, and the man collapsed forward.

George shouted, "Hold, Angel, hold!" The dog wrenched the man's arm sideways a few more times before letting go.

"Hav'n' a picnic here in da woods? My dog don' take kindly to trespassers."

"We's just rest'n' back here. Keep that beast away from me!"

"I see yer friends took my horse. Those two yours?"

He nodded his head.

"What's yer name?"

"Orville Stanton. We didn't mean you no harm."

"You a good Christian man, Mister Orville Stanton?"

"I am, truly. Jesus Christ is my Lord and Savior."

"What you think he's gonna do about you kill'n' a old woman in front o' her home?"

"It weren't me. I didn't know they'd shoot her. She's dead afore I could move."

"And how's your Savior gonna feel about yer plans to burn us alive? Must be a special place in hell for some'n who'd do dat. You must like flames, Mister Orville Stanton."

"We weren't really go'n' to do it. Please let me go."

"Well, Jesus'll be real happy to hear dat."

"When he asks who brought you to him, you tell Jesus it was, Lazarus. Lazarus George. Enjoy the flames."

He fired his pistol point blank into Orville's chest.

George and Colin looked at each other, breathing hard, acknowledging their situation. George cocked his head toward the shack, and Colin followed him to where Constance lay. "Cain't leave her here." He lifted her with two strong arms, carried her back into the shack, and stood at the corner near the crawl space. Colin understood. He cleared the boards and helped place her gently underground.

George knelt to pray. Colin did likewise, asking God to accept her soul in gratitude for all she had done, and praying that her daughter could live her life in freedom.

George tugged Colin's shoulder and gestured toward the door. Colin followed him to where the two men lay. "Help me get em into da house." Together, they dragged the bodies inside. "Check der pockets." Colin searched, finding some money and keys, nothing significant. "You steady da horses. I'm gonna torch dis place."

Flames fully engulfed the shack as they mounted up and rode north through the woods.

Reunion

"We can travel through da night. But likely have to hide out afore sunup."

"Heading northeast is probably safest. Do you really not know where the armies are now?"

"You think the army tells me der plans?" Gesturing toward the rising moon, then swinging his arm up halfway and pointing. "Dis way."

Riding was hard on Colin's left leg; it didn't have strength to grip properly. He wasn't much of a horseman and worried what might happen if the animal got spooked. Angel trotted along next to them, their early warning system in the event of trouble ahead.

Both men were nearly asleep in their saddles as the sun pierced the far horizon. Their trek had taken them out of the forest and along a widening stream. Angel trotted down the embankment to take a drink. The activity stirred George. He knew the horses needed water too and brought them to a stop. That's when he noticed blood trickling from Colin's leg.

"Whoa, Colin, you bleed'n' again."

Colin opened his eyes, bending over to see what George meant. His pant leg was red with blood. The stitches must have torn. The bleeding was light, but troubling. He brought his horse to a stop, and George helped him down.

Colin limped toward the river. He sat on a rock, removing his boot, and pulled up his pant leg to see where the threads had come undone. George wet a cloth from his saddlebag and gently patted the wound. He unclipped Colin's canteen and offered him a drink. The horses were bending low, lapping their fill, when George noticed small patches of smoke from the far side of the stream. Together, they smelled coffee and baked bread. Voices could be heard, too distant to know what they said.

"You wait here. I'll see."

George bent low as he moved across the stream and into the bushes on the other side. He returned a few minutes later, jubilant.

"They's Union troops! You better go ahead so I don't startle' em."

He helped Colin on with his boot and supported him as they crossed to the other side. Walking unannounced into a soldiers' camp during wartime could be dangerous, so Colin started singing *The Battle Hymn of the Republic*: "Mine eyes have seen the glory …" They emerged slowly from the bushes and were greeted by a ragtag group of sleepy Union soldiers.

In short order, he was ushered into a command tent. Colonel Morris listened to Colin's story, confirmed he'd been listed as dead, and had a corpsman look at his wounds. "First time I've seen someone shot in the leg who didn't lose it. How you avoided infection's a mystery to me. You may consider your service to this war concluded."

Morris arranged for the appropriate paperwork and even had Colin visit the purser to receive a month's pay.

"Can you write?"

"I can."

"Put down what you want to tell your family and how to reach them. I'll have a telegram sent right away."

***

Warren and Mary paced the station platform, desperate to see him again. Warren harbored a fear the telegram might have been a cruel joke. They were surprised when a large German Shepherd trotted onto the platform ahead of Colin. Warren didn't care how fierce the dog looked; he rushed to embrace his son.

Mary followed close on his heels. Colin turned his head away, hiding his scar. The three of them held each other and laughed and cried. A tall Negro stood behind him.

Colin stiffened, turned, and introduced George and Angel as his rescuers. He briefly explained all they had done for him, and Warren gave George a handshake and a thankful hug.

"I am forever in your debt."

Mary bent down and hugged Angel. "Such an appropriate name for your dog. He's a saint!"

"He was called Satan at one time, but that's a long story."

Mary stood, placing her hand on Colin's cheek, gently fingering his scar. He turned away again, but she brought his head forward, looked in his eyes and smiled.

"It's a mark of distinction. Too bad so much of it'll be covered by hair. A war wound'll get you a lot of drinks from me brothers' crowd."

As they rode home, Colin took in every detail of Boston: the architecture, people at their daily tasks, the familiar sights, sounds and smells he'd taken for granted before. The city felt more precious with every block. He was home.

Warren had the guest room made up for George and, with some trepidation, permitted the dog to stay with him there. Dinner that night was a feast. Warren had been planning the homecoming celebration ever since the telegram arrived. The war was still going poorly, but he had his son home. His business was flourishing with war contracts generating more business than they could keep up. All was right with the world.

After dinner, Colin and Mary went for a carriage ride. He held her hand and told her something she hadn't expected: "I've had a lot of time to think about the future." She shifted closer and squeezed his hand. "As soon as I know the business is doing well, I'm going to leave."

She sat upright and took her hand out of his. Mary paused, looking in to his eyes.

"You've just come home. Your Da'll be devastated. He ..."

"Not leaving Boston, just the business. I want to start a school, teach music. A school for the less fortunate."

"Like your precious St. Anne's?"

"Of a sort, yes. I thought you should know because, as my wife, you'll be Head Mistress of the school."

"Is that a fact, then? I'll be yer wife without e'en so much as a proposal? The knock to yer head did more damage than I supposed." She punched his arm.

He turned to face her. "I'm an idiot! I'm so sorry. Please forgive me, Mary. You have all my heart, and all my thoughts. I've spent every day thinking I'd spend the rest of my life with you, and I realize now, I never asked."

"Don't be rush'n' into anythin'. 'Tis not the time, and you've nae been home long enough to make a sensible decision. Especially about leav'n' your Da. You're the resurrected son, and I won't have ya break'n' his heart."

"I only mean to do it if the business is secure."

"You are an idiot. He's not runn'n' the business fer himself! His entire dream is to build something you'd be secure in, somth'n' to keep ya worry-free fer the rest of yer life. Don't be turn'n" his gift aside so casually."

"You're right. I ..."

A long silence ensued until they were almost home.

"So, tell me now, what's yer plan for this school?"

***

Warren was getting used to a dog in the house. He brought sheets and towels up to George's room, along with a set of clean clothes. "You'll be wanting something fresher now that you've bathed, I suppose."

George was sitting on the bed, pushing on the mattress with his hands to judge its firmness. Angel slept on the floor next to him, but his ears picked up when Warren entered. The dog turned his head to face Warren, who froze for a second.

"No need to do noth'n' fer me. Place to rest my head is welcome enough."

"I owe you everything. You brought my son home to me. Stay in Boston. I'll give you work and pay enough to provide a good living for you. You'll have a life of freedom here."

"Dat sounds powerfully good, Mr. Phelps. But I got people in the south need'n' weapons and support." He took off his shirt to try on the one Warren had given him. "First clean clothes fer as long as I kin remember."

Warren told him he was welcome to all the clean clothes he'd ever want when he noticed the star branded on George's shoulder. After a long silence, he said, "You saved Colin in Maryland. Was that your home? Do you have family there?"

"No, suh. Home was Georgia. Parents are each dead. I had a sister once, but she disappeared in Cuba. We got captured there. A sea captain came in to where we was held. Pulled my sister out, and we never seen her again. I 'spect he kept her. Anyway, it's just me now."

Warren drew in a quick breath, swallowing hard, his face flushed. He stared at George's branded shoulder, then looked closely into his eyes before turning away. He might not recognize George as that slave boy from so long ago, but George might recognize him. Warren made a quick excuse and headed downstairs.

The next morning at breakfast, Warren watched George carefully. It was apparent the young man didn't remember him at all. He struck a bargain with George. He would employ him for a month and pay him a significant wage that would allow him to finance guns and equipment to slaves. His offer was accepted.

Colin slowly got back into the daily experience of returning to work. He took pride in showing George every aspect of the business. George was a quick learner and even came up with suggestions to lower costs and organize tasks more efficiency. He exhibited a natural aptitude for mechanics.

George agreed to stay in Boston for at least a month. He enjoyed learning the business, being part of decision-making. He even thought of staying longer, but his commitment to arming slaves was paramount. All that changed a few weeks later when Abraham Lincoln announced he would issue the Emancipation Proclamation. Slaves in Confederate states would be free.

"No reason to arm the slaves now. They'll be free in January, and our troops are already turning the tide. Besides, you're valuable here. I want you to stay."

Warren took George to lunch at the Union Oyster House.

"This is where Colin and I had our first lunch in Boston. I thought it an appropriate place to discuss an opportunity with you. I owe you more than I can repay, and I hope to persuade you to stay. Your work at the factory has already proved impressive."

"Thank you, but I got folks d'pend'n' on me down south."

"Exactly. And I fear for what will become of them, newly emancipated, coming off the fields with little or no skills, owning no land of their own. Here's my idea: stay with us, allow me to teach you a trade. Our business involves a number of unique skills, each with its own tradesmanship. You have a strong aptitude and could flourish in any of those trades."

"I 'preciate dat, but ..."

"Hear me out. As you learn those skills, you'll not only make a living for yourself, you'll be able to teach former slaves how to fare for themselves. Colin told me about your friend Joe. I'm sure we could use his talents at Phelps Industries. If you stay, we can work together to help lift your brethren up."

George had to admit Warren's proposal offered an opportunity he couldn't forsake. The arrangement was sealed over a dessert of cranberry pie.

Colin introduced George to Rebecca and her family. She, in turn, introduced him to other free blacks in Boston. He built a solid community.

When Colin did formally propose to Mary, he did it well, with a significant amount of advance preparation. He took her to another concert on the Commons, seated in the front row, close to the orchestra.

Just before intermission, the conductor announced they would play a new song by a promising young Boston composer, a gentleman by the name of Colin Phelps.

Mary looked shocked. He gave her a broad smile as he rose to take the stage.

Colin took his seat at the piano bench and announced he would be playing a song he called "Mary of My Heart." It began with soft steady chords. Violins flowed in, followed by oboes, French horns, and percussion. The music picked up the pace. It was light and beautiful: one section paid homage to Irish dance tunes before repeating a high glorious stanza, drifting back to gentle pulsing beats, and ending almost quietly. The audience was impressed, giving the composer enthusiastic applause and a standing ovation.

As Colin left the stage to join her, George appeared with the biggest bouquet of flowers she had ever seen. Colin took it and gave it her, bending on one knee as he produced a small black jewelry box.

"Mary, you *are* my heart. Will you do me the great honor of bestowing your hand to me in marriage?"

She laughed through tears, nodded her head and said, "I might as well, since ya won't be giv'n' up."

Another standing ovation.

Her brothers had been hidden farther back in the audience. They approached, circling the couple, with hugs and greetings for all.

George was his best man. The reception turned lively when Mary and her girls took turns teaching step-dancing to Colin, George, and a few other young men. Most were well lubricated before the start of the dance, attempting to click their heels to the fast motion of the music, creating a comical scene with more than one participant falling to the floor.

Their wedding night was enjoyed in one of Boston's finest hotels. The following morning, Colin took Mary on a stroll along the Charles River across from Harvard. He pointed to the college.

"This is why I want to start our school. That institution is a gateway to the world. It educates some of the wealthiest children in the Union. But it's locked shut to those who struggle, to the poor, to women. We need to give a hand up to the less fortunate."

"What would we call it?"

"I was thinking, The Promise School."

And Then

Warren was content with life again. Business was going well, he had the hope of grandchildren before too long, and George was proving a valuable addition to his company.

He was unprepared, but understood, when Colin asked to leave the business, insisting his heart was set on starting the school.

Furthermore, Colin asked that George be made a permanent part of Phelps Industries. Warren had no disagreement with that. He owed everything to George. Colin proposed that George be given 20 percent of the business. Colin would keep 20 percent, and Warren would retain 60 percent.

Colin and Mary invited George to supper to celebrate the new year, and also because Colin had something to propose.

"I've been thinking about Constance. She saved both our lives. Neither of us would be here without her."

"She was a proud, powerful woman. God's heal'n' angel."

"Constance told me about her daughter, about Elizabeth."

"Broke her heart when they took dat girl!"

"It occurs to me, with the war over, maybe she could be found. She said her girl was given to a cousin. Do you have any idea who that might have been?"

"That was Abigail. I seen her at the Price place two er three times. A frivolous l'l thing carn'n' only fer fashion and society. Mind as empty as an Easter tomb. Married real well though. Constance wud a loved to see dis day. She and I had it all planned out, learned where they lived, figured how we was gonna get her after da war."

Colin stood up, "I think we should still do it. It's what Constance would want."

George's eyebrows went up, a smile turned into laughter. He extended his hand for Colin to shake. "Powerful good idea," clapping Colin's shoulders with both hands, "I guess we's gonna do it!"

It was a long and dangerous trip. No one wanted a Yankee, particularly one accompanied by three northerners and a Negro, asking questions about other people's former property. But they did find her. She was twenty-eight years old, thin, looking more like forty, still living on the same farm. Abigail's husband had died during the war. The property was quickly falling into disrepair. Elizabeth remained only because she had no place else to go.

She didn't remember her mother but was fascinated by descriptions of how she had brought George and Colin back to life. Elizabeth accompanied them to Boston, where they found employment for her in a bakery at a decent wage. She lived with Rebecca and her children for three years before taking a husband and starting a family of her own.

Colin was the best man at George's wedding, served as godfather to his first son, and insisted that all five of George's children attend The Promise School. They remained close friends throughout their lives.

Over the years, George became a 60 percent owner of the business, inheriting the balance of his shares from a grateful Warren on his demise. He officially changed his name to George Sherman, after the general who liberated Georgia's slaves.

Mr. Sherman became a well-respected pillar of the Boston business community, a frequent speaker at civic events, a mentor for younger blacks, and a writer whose memoir was widely read and acclaimed. Every June he was a featured lecturer at Colin's school, teaching children about slavery and all he had endured.

Mary and Colin raised seven children: four girls and three boys. Each was educated in, and each helped out at the Promise School.

It became a steppingstone for the less fortunate, providing quality education and family support, giving Boston's poorer youths a chance to compete against more privileged students. The Promise Choir earned a widespread respectable reputation.

As Headmistress, Mary made sure the school was run properly. She devoted her life to its students, becoming a surrogate mother to many with encouragement, gentle discipline, and loving guidance. Naturally, she also served as the school's dance instructor. It was often suggested that the school be renamed the Mary Dowling Promise School.

For their twenty-fifth wedding anniversary, Colin and Mary took a tour of England and Ireland. Colin's most treasured time was their visit to St. Anne's. He met with the new headmaster, Father Sedgwick, and toured the school. He and Mary attended a performance of the Boys Choir at Albert Hall. The school had grown nicely, and the choir exceeded even Colin's highest expectations.

Father Sedgwick said how grateful the school was for all that Colin's father had provided. "The gifts continued after his death. I presume you are our benefactor now?"

"I can't say that I am."

"Can't say, or won't say?"

"I can only say my heart soars to see St. Anne's prospering so well."

If Father McCall was right that every second on earth, every decision and action, falls on one side of the scale or the other, and that every moment is preserved forever in memory, Colin's eternal joy in heaven was assured.

AUTHOR'S NOTES

THE Civil War finally ended in May 1865. On December 6th, the Thirteenth Amendment to the Constitution was ratified, abolishing slavery throughout the country. William Lloyd Garrison published his last edition of *The Liberator* on December 29th.

Ironically, had the Confederate States stayed in the Union and joined the northern states who had already ratified the Corwin Amendment, slavery would have been made a permanent part of the Constitution without another shot being fired.

The language in the California Resolution referenced in *The Liberator* chapter is an actual word-for-word repetition of the bill introduced in that state's lower House. It drove my spell check function to the brink of exhaustion.

St. Anne's Church and its choir are real. The church was consecrated in 1686. Its choir and organ music were cherished from their outset and heralded for the first UK performance of Bach's "St. John's Passion." St. Anne's played royal performances for Queen Victoria at Windsor Castle and at Buckingham Palace for Queen Alexandra. I've not yet visited there.

I've heard stories my grandfather, Michael Joseph Kelley, newly arrived from Ireland, often helped friends "shop" for decent coats in exactly the manner described in the Shopping for a Friend chapter.

Abby Kelley is a true historical figure, who devoted her life to women's rights and the abolition of slavery. While we share the same last name, we are, sadly, not related.

The solar flares that lit the skies in 1859 actually happened.

Anonymous payments from the Bank of England to Amanda Winters of 1047 Abington Trace continued throughout Warren's life. The deposits were uninterrupted because it was an obligation he never entrusted to Joseph Newton. She eventually overcame her grief at the loss of her sea captain husband and married a respected judge.

While this novel portrays real historical characters and events as its backdrop, the main characters herein did not exist.

I am grateful to my editors Elsi Dodge and Christine Howard for all their help and suggestions.

Thank You for Your Gift to Charity

All proceeds from the sale of this book will be divided equally between two Colorado charities:

Attention Homes (now TGTR), which has provided care and guidance to homeless and at-risk teens in Boulder, Colorado, for over fifty years, and the Colorado Women's Education Foundation (CWEF), which provides scholarships to women who are non-traditional college students, often single mothers or the first woman ever to enter college in their family.

You can find more information on both of them at:

https://tgtr.org

https://cwef.org

Before You Go:

As a beginning author, I'd be grateful for your comments and especially thankful if you write a review on Amazon.

ENJOY TWO CHAPTERS OF MY NOVEL,

A TIME OF LIES, ON THE NEXT PAGES.

CNN WASHINGTON, DC 2007

CHRISTIANE **Amanpour**: "Okay, Brandon, cameras are rolling. I know these lights are bright. Just look at me or into the camera and you'll be fine. In a few seconds, I'll get a signal to start. I'll make a brief introduction and then give you a chance to tell your side of the story. Are you ready?"

Brandon: "I think so."

Christiane: "All right. Here we go: Good evening, I'm Christiane Amanpour with a CNN exclusive interview. I'm sitting here with Brandon McCarty, brother of Lieutenant Brian McCarty.

"Despite everything we've seen and heard about Lt. McCarty this month, Brandon remains convinced of his brother's innocence.

"Brandon, there's every indication your brother betrayed our country. Why should we believe what you have to say is anything other than family loyalty in the face of overwhelming evidence? How do you respond to that?"

Brandon: "Look, I understand why people are angry, I've seen the same footage, but they're wrong. They don't know my brother; they don't know the half of it. I know his heart, and I can tell you Brian McCarty loves America and would never do anything to harm it.

"Suddenly, he's accused of treason, his career and reputation are ruined; his wife and child are under siege. Our own mother can't even leave the house without reporters converging on her like a pack of wolves.

"It's completely unfair. No matter what you see in those videos. It's snap judgment, and it's wrong. I just wish people knew his side of the story."

SEPTEMBER MOURN – 2001

BRIAN McCarty's second class at Darien High School had just started. The clock on the pale blue cinderblock wall read nine-twelve when three shrill blasts sounded over the PA system. An assembly was announced with attendance mandatory, no exceptions. *Good*, he thought, *I'll miss calculus.*

He grabbed his backpack and joined the stream of students heading to the auditorium, surprised to see two teachers running to the theater. He stood taller, extending his six-foot height, scanning over students' heads, then picked up his pace, weaving in and out of groups of classmates, feeling tension roll through the hallway.

Students were barely inside when Principal Hanley tapped the microphone forcefully with his fingers, spread his arms, hands flapping, urging silence from the podium.

"I know many of you have family working in the city. You should know there's been an attack on the World Trade Center."

Brian listened as Hanley explained what little he knew about the planes and the towers, and announced school was closed for the day. He sat for a few seconds, letting it sink in. He wasn't sure how close his father's office was to the World Trade Center, but knew the Financial District had to be near enough.

He launched out of his seat, running into the hallway, looking for anyone who could give him a ride. Mark Herndon had almost reached the parking lot when Brian poked him on the shoulder.

"Can I get a ride? I need to check on my mom."

Mark laughed. "Hey, relax. It's a day off! Let's go someplace fun."

"No! I can't. My dad works in Manhattan. I really need to get home."

"Sorry, I forgot. Come on."

A faint scent of breakfast still lingered when Brian opened the kitchen door: a mix of coffee, toast, and bacon. Scooter bounded into the room, skidding across the tile floor, wagging his tail and jumping up for his usual hug. It all felt comforting, until he saw his mother in the den staring at the television, a phone to her ear, her voice wavering:

"But somebody must know *something*!"

After a pause, she said, "Call me as soon as you know. I'm switching to my cell to keep our landline open." She looked up at Brian and beckoned him to her side.

"Oh, God," she said, reaching out, giving him a long tight hug. She stepped back, resting a hand on his shoulder, her eyes darting past him, as if willing her husband to walk through the door. "I've been calling him, but I can't get through.

"We don't know anything yet," ... still staring at the door. "His office is closing; everyone's being evacuated. They aren't sure where your father is. He's scheduled for a meeting at Cantor Fitzgerald." Her head turned toward the television, then swung back to her son. "Brian ... their office is in one of those towers."

Brian swallowed hard as he realized the implications. The room squeezed in. He looked at her expression, clenched his fists and thought: *This is insane! Why would anybody do this? Who's doing this?*

He watched his mother sink into a chair, her eyes fixed on the television. She leapt when the phone rang. Brian thought it must be his dad. But it wasn't him, or his office. It was his aunt in Illinois calling his mother to see if she'd heard the news, calling to see if Tom was safe. His mother rushed the conversation to clear the line. It occurred to Brian that she'd get several such calls, and all he wanted was an open line so his dad could get through. He checked to make sure his own cell was fully charged, then called his dad's number. No answer. He tried again.

They waited forty-five minutes, with no word. A reporter said people had been seen leaping from the upper floors. His mother stiffened her back and stood directly in front of the television, her fingers over her mouth, her eyes fixed. She reached back awkwardly, grabbing her son's hand without taking her eyes off the screen. Brian moved beside her, looping an arm around her shoulders, feeling helpless, not knowing how to comfort her, not taking his own eyes off the set.

Thick gray-white smoke streamed from the towers, billowing high overhead while rescue crews rushed urgently about. Church bells tolled in the background. More news: The Pentagon had been hit. An airliner was missing over Pennsylvania and presumed down. All flights were grounded. The President was in Florida, reading to children at an elementary school. It felt surreal. Nobody seemed in charge; no one could explain a reason for the attack or even who the attackers were. He should be in high school preparing for gym; now he watched a nation under attack, perhaps preparing for war.

Just before ten o'clock his mother let out a shriek. The first tower collapsed, floor by floor, until its entire mass hit the street, spewing enormous clouds of heavy gray smoke. Concrete dust and debris flashed in concentric circles, encasing everything under a thick pulsing blanket, choking off air. Terrified people emerged from the smoke: gray ghosts, gasping for air, running for their lives. A woman fell onto the street. No one stopped to help.

Brian's mother squeezed his arm tightly, turning to him, her mouth open, her eyes wide in horror. Flames and smoke streamed from the upper floors of the second tower. A reporter said, "There's incomprehensible mayhem in the streets; it looks like New York is in the midst of a nuclear winter."

When the second tower collapsed, his mother collapsed with it.

Noon came without a word. Brian's brothers had each called. Ted, a doctor in Madison, Wisconsin, called from his office. He offered to drive straight home, since flights had been grounded. "Not yet," Brian said. "I'm sure we'll hear something soon." Brandon, at the London School of Economics, hoping to follow his father into finance, called, expecting to hear his dad was fine, and was shocked to learn that might not be the case. Again, Brian said, "Let's just wait. I'll call as soon as I know something." Each brother spoke briefly with their mother, but she was too fragile to carry on much of a conversation.

Brian couldn't bear waiting. He grabbed a photo of his father from the grand piano, sliding the picture out of its frame, intending to run copies on the home printer. His hands shook; an image of his father lying trapped under concrete flashed in his head.

"Brian, what are you doing?"

"I'm gonna find Dad. If he can't reach us, I'll find someone who's seen him."

He thought his father must be helping people, too busy to call. Besides, most phones were still down. Of course he'd be helping others. If nothing else, Tom McCarty had a strong sense of Catholic guilt that fueled a willingness to help others. He believed in the rewards of heaven.

She let out a heavy sigh and stood up, wringing her hands. "No. Stay! Please wait. He'll call."

"I can't just sit here, Mom. I've got to do something!"

He turned toward the door, but she blocked his way, putting both hands on his arms and locking his eyes with hers.

"Please, I need you here. I can't wait by myself." His mother sagged, and Brian had to keep her from falling. She steadied one hand on the piano as he helped her to the sofa. Scooter placed his head on her lap, his brown eyes looking up at her, concerned, his tail slowly thumping the floor, offering encouragement. She absently stroked his fur.

"It's okay, Mom. I'll stay. I'm sure you're right. Dad will be fine. He'll call as soon as the lines are open."

Something fundamental had changed. It hadn't occurred to him that his mother might need him. It had always been the other way around. Of course, he would wait with her for the call.

At six o'clock Brian knelt beside his bed, praying earnestly through tears, prayers interspersed with sharp bouts of anger, his fists pounding the bed, while light drained from the room. His mind swirled with images of his father trapped under twisted steel or, worse, scattering as ash, drifting over the city.

The call never came. His brothers returned home to Connecticut. His aunt flew in from Chicago and stayed nearly two weeks. His mother was too fragile to cope with even the smallest daily task.

The memorial service was held at St. John's Parish. Tom had been an usher there every Sunday, and Brian had been an altar boy in middle school. Their church overflowed with mourners.

Monsignor gave a warm eulogy, speaking from the heart, of Tom's devotion to family and to the Lord. Brian was taken aback when the priest actually used the words, "Ashes to ashes and dust to dust." He didn't appreciate the phrase. He thought of the enormous clouds of ash and dust spewing from the towers and thought, "Part of that was my dad."

But then the priest said, "Take heart. We will all see Tom again. He is gone but a little while. As Jesus said in the Book of John, 'There are many rooms in my Father's house; I go there to prepare one for you.' We will see Tom again, waiting for us, fully restored, in the complete joy of heaven."

Of all the souls who lost their lives that day, 156 were from Connecticut. There were two services in Tom's memory and a host of group services in both Connecticut and Manhattan for all the victims. Brian wished they would stop. He wished his family didn't have to be reminded of their loss every day. Not that he could ever forget, but they all needed space to recover.

He felt hopelessly lost. The sound of his father's voice came to him at odd hours, every day, like a tape recording playing endlessly in his head:

"Brian, there's a reason people get discouraged with the world. They expect great things from it, and when it doesn't happen, they give up. Don't assume the world will do great things for you. Demand great things from yourself and make your own world great."

His father's death created a deep void he began filling with anger and determination. Within days, one clear, overpowering resolve formed in Brian's heart. He would not let this stand. He would devote his life to protecting his country. He was fully committed to getting into a military academy. West Point was closer to home, but he preferred the Naval Academy at Annapolis.

He began a new physical regimen. Already in decent shape from soccer, he dedicated himself to peak performance, waking up at four-thirty each morning Monday through Saturday. At first, he ran four miles, increased it to five and finally six miles a day. After school, he used the gym to bulk up, lifting weights, doing sit-ups, leg lifts, and push-ups. Each week he increased the number of reps, feeling his strength and endurance grow. If he made the Academy, he wanted to be prepared for all its physical demands.

Leaving the house early on dark, crisp mornings while the stars still sparkled made him feel alive. Scooter ran at his side, pulling the leash sideways whenever rabbits or squirrels darted from bushes. Toward the end of his run, lights would appear in some of the homes. Husbands and wives shuffling into the kitchen to start coffee, parents waking sleepy children. He felt the presence of his father, and a fierce determination to make him proud.

Principal Hanley, along with half the faculty at Darien High, wrote glowing letters to their congressman and two senators. Nothing pleased an elected official more than nominating the son of a 9/11 victim to a military academy. Competition arose to nominate

Brian. Senator Blumenthal's staff was more efficient, and Brian's nomination formally came from his office.

The senator made a special trip to Darien, appearing with Brian to announce the Naval Academy had officially accepted his nomination. Soon, Brian McCarty would be a midshipman on his way to becoming either an ensign in the Navy or a second lieutenant in the Marines. Everyone felt so proud. No one could have predicted the path his life would take.

Kevin's Other Novels

A Time of Lies

Historical fiction: A novel of romance and adventure. A love affair is shattered when a Naval Intelligence Officer finds himself in North Korea. "Consequences? Will America launch an attack against the invincible Korean military, for a traitor? Will they risk that against one million Korean soldiers? I think not. You are here for life. You must decide how long that life will be."

A Time of Chaos

An assassination on Inauguration Day is the first in a series of disasters challenging Vice President Cahill who suddenly becomes Commander-in-Chief. The security of the country is at risk and a march to war seems inevitable. Has the real threat gone undetected? Is any secret safe in the White House?

A Time of Ever After

Mr. Sinclair is locked securely in Colorado's Supermax prison. But it's hard to keep a bad man down. A new time of chaos ensues.

Available on Amazon in Kindle and paperback.

I'm grateful for feedback. Please feel free to contact me at:

kevinkelleyis@gmail.com

About the Author

Kevin and his wife, Ronda, live in Colorado. His writing draws from an extensive background of real-world experience. He lived in Germany, England, and Belgium while growing up. His careers included five years as a Legislative Assistant to a high-ranking member of Congress, five years as the Federal Relations Liaison for the City of Boston, heading their DC office, and over twenty years as an Investment Advisor.

He's involved with several non-profit organizations and cherishes the time he can set aside to write.

Kevin has been active in his church, serving as an elder, treasurer, trustee, and Sunday School teacher to fourth and fifth graders.

He's the proud father of three children and proud Papa to three grandchildren.

Made in the USA
Coppell, TX
23 June 2024